SON OF MAN

Retelling the Stories of Jesus

CHARLES MARTIN

W PUBLISHING GROUP

AN IMPRINT OF THOMAS NELSON

ISBN 978-1-4003-3353-0 (eBook)
ISBN 978-1-4003-3354-7 (audiobook)

Library of Congress Cataloging-in-Publication Data on File

ISBN 978-1-4003-3352-3

Printed in the United States of America

22 23 24 25 26 LSC 10 9 8 7 6 5 4 3 2 1

CONTENTS

Introduction v

Entering the Courtroom 1

God with Us 9

Daughter of God 25

Only Believe 33

In the Power of Jesus 37

The Good Confession 45

Neither Do I Condemn You 49

Where the Father's Love Found Him 51

The Signature of the Messiah 57

By This 65

The Covenant 69

Betrayed 73

King of the Jews 79

The Father's Silence 87

Propitiation 93

Enter the King of Glory 103

The Borrowed Tomb 109

Can It Be? 113

On the Road to Emmaus 123

The Do-Over 127

What Next? 135

The Helper Comes 145

Fearless 157

Blinded to See 161

The Banquet of the Ages 167

Endnotes 179

INTRODUCTION

He can't fix this mess. He stares down at the road below him and knows, beyond a shadow of any doubt, he is powerless to do anything about anything. The consequences of his life's choices have caught up with him. Right here. He's a criminal. Draped in regret. Convicted of multiple crimes. His sentence is crucifixion. This is literally the end of the road. Sometime today, or tonight, his life will end. He's not sure how long he'll last. But given that Sabbath is a few hours away, he's pretty sure the soldiers will break his legs with that heavy iron bar, and he won't be able to push up to breathe. The clock ticks. It's not long now.

He is hanging on a cross outside of Jerusalem, AD 33. To his right hangs his friend. Or at least a fellow criminal. I doubt they're friends as much as partners in crime.

Between them is a man he's never met. But the man must have done something awfully wrong because He is shredded like burger. Nothing remains of His back, sides, and shoulders. In fact, He doesn't even look like a man. And while our criminal is tied to his cross, the man in the middle has been nailed to His. Hands and feet. Whatever happened to the man on the middle cross prior to His arrival here must have been horrific because it looks as if all His bones are out of joint. Above His head a sign reads "King of the Jews," but judging by the mocking shouts of those surrounding Him, few believe it.

The soldiers seem to be enjoying themselves. They spit on the man in the middle. Gamble for His clothes. And one of the soldiers takes a sponge on a stick, called a *tersorium*, dips it in feces-laced vinegar, and shoves it into His mouth. The man doesn't like it. He is struggling to remain conscious, and it appears the weight of the world is hanging on His shoulders.

The man speaks in Aramaic. Suggesting He's a Galilean. A Hebrew. A woman, evidently the man's mother, approaches. He says something to her. She cries on the shoulder of another man. That her heart is pierced is obvious.

Now the man is praying. Talking to God. He calls Him *Father*. They must know each other because it sounds as if He's done that before. A lot.

The second criminal is indignant. Cussing the man on

the middle cross. Railing. "Are you not the Christ? Save yourself and us!"

The first thief rebukes the second. "Do you not fear God since you are under the same sentence of condemnation? And we indeed justly, for we are receiving the due reward of our deeds . . ." His words tell us much about him.

For starters, he's telling the truth. Sees himself clearly. No more lies. He got what he deserved. But not the man in the middle. Then he says, "Jesus, remember me when You come into Your kingdom."

Hold it.

Why does he say this? What happened? There are two criminals. One on Jesus' left. One on His right. One believes. One mocks. They're both looking at the same Jesus. What gives?

Here's what I think. Early in His earthly ministry, Jesus said, "As Moses lifted up the serpent in the wilderness, even so must the Son of Man be lifted up, that whoever believes in Him should not perish but have eternal life."[1] This comes just before the most famous verse in the Bible.

Back up briefly. The Israelites have made their exodus. Left Egypt. Now they're wandering the desert. Complaining. Cussing God, "Things were better when we were slaves." God sends snakes to bite them. Many die. Then God speaks the remedy, "Make a bronze serpent and put it on a pole. Everyone who looks at it will be healed and not die."

The condition was that you had to come forward, look up, admit you are the cause of your own sickness, and confess you can't fix you. God alone can. Looking up was an outward expression of an inward condition. Humility. "I did this. I sinned. Forgive me, please."

It's a picture of repentance.

According to Jesus, God was setting up the conditions for our return to Himself. Jesus must be lifted up. Crucified. Which is happening right next to our criminal. The single most important day in human history, and he has a front-row seat.

My question is this: How does he believe and the other criminal not? What happened to move his heart from not believing to believing?

Well, according to Scripture, God got tired of his not believing and did a thing in his heart. But let's look closer at what we see. Right there, just a few feet away, before his very eyes, hangs Jesus. *The* Son of God.

And two words reveal the thief's heart: *Your kingdom.*

We have no idea what he thought or believed about this Jesus prior, but in that moment, he believes Jesus is who the sign above His head declares Him to be. *The* Son of God. *The* King with a kingdom. And that today, after some time of absence, He's returning to it.

This belief that Jesus is who He says He is, is probably not the thinking that landed the thief on that cross. But of all the people in Scripture, of all the saints, we know something about this criminal that cannot be said of any other saint or person in Scripture. We know, beyond a shadow of a doubt, that He is with Jesus. Right this second. "Assuredly, I say to you, today you will be with Me in Paradise."[2]

What has the thief done to earn this?

He's not gone to church. Hasn't amended his ways or paid back all he owes. He hasn't studied great theological truths. Hasn't joined a discipleship group. Hasn't served at his local church. Hasn't visited the prisoners. Hasn't fed the poor. Hasn't taken care of widows and orphans. He can't even lift his hands in worship because they're tied to the crossbar. This dude hasn't done squat and yet, according to Jesus, this criminal is in heaven as I write this.

Which means there's hope for us.

This inexplicable thing that Jesus does—this grace, this unmerited mercy, this salvation, this snatching back out of the hand of the devil—is a gift beyond measure. We can't earn it and don't deserve it. In fact, every one of us deserves the very crucifixion Jesus suffers. But for reasons I cannot fathom, He hangs there.

So let's go back a few steps. What happened? Just yesterday, the criminal was . . . a criminal. He got caught, had a trial, was convicted, marched out of town, and unceremoniously hung on this tree. And by his own admission, he deserves it. What happened between yesterday and right now?

I think the answer lies in the criminal's view. His perspective. Look through his eyes. Watch what he's watching. The man on the middle cross is drowning in his own lung fluid. Now listen with his ears. "Father, forgive them." "I thirst." "Mother, behold your son." Now smell with his nose. He's outside the town, out where they burn the trash. He's also close enough to smell Jesus' sweat and blood.

In this moment, Jesus is anything but kingly. Or is He?

Throughout Scripture, whenever someone encounters Jesus, they see something—or someone—they've never seen. They see themselves in relation to Him. And there's no comparison. They fall on their faces and want to crawl into a hole. Disappear. They use words like *unclean* and *not worthy*. The juxtaposition is a chasm they can't cross. They can't wrap their minds around Him.

You and I have a problem. And while there is great disagreement among most people about most things on planet Earth, most will agree that things here are broken. And they're not getting better. No ruler, no leader, no guru has been able to or can fix us. We are like fruit. Left to ourselves, we rot. You can stick us in the fridge for a period of time, but that only slows the rotting.

The cause? It's not that world leader with his finger on a button. It's not this or that political party. It's not this or that judicial ruling. It's not this or that people group, not this or that nightly news channel, and it's not your neighbor who doesn't pick up after their dog. It's a little closer to home. And, unfortunately, it resides in every one of us.

That one thing is sin. That's our singular problem. Sin.

We're all snakebit. From birth. The poison flows in our veins, and the only antivenom is the shed blood of Jesus. Period.

I'm all for good leaders, just laws, truth in our channels, and friendly neighbors, but even if we had all that, we'd still be broken. We can't fix us. We've proven that. If we could have, we would have. Despite how smart we think we are, there is no intellectual system or approach that will get us back to good. While we were created for Eden, we don't live there and won't live there until Jesus returns and ushers in a new heaven and a new earth. Until then, we're stuck with the problem.

And sin—all sin—must be paid for. Cleansed. Purged. Removed. God won't tolerate it.

Free of the veil, the thief hangs on the cross, wishes he could scratch his head, and realizes, maybe for the first time, that he is at fault: "I'm a sinner, and judging by the marks on His mutilated body, the problem is worse than I think. I couldn't fix me in ten thousand lifetimes. I don't need a self-help book or a life coach, and no amount of money will pay my debt. I need a savior. Period."

Jesus said, "I am the way, the truth, and the life. No one comes to the Father except through Me."[3] And hanging there, listening to Jesus gurgle, the thief knows this.

The light bulb turns on. Blindfold removed. With only a few breaths remaining, the thief realizes Jesus is the only way out of this mess. Jesus said, "And I, if I am lifted up from the earth, will draw all peoples to Myself."[4] And that moment of lifting and drawing happens before the criminal's eyes. Literally. He is watching sin, all sin, throughout all eternity—past, present, future—for all mankind, be paid for. Wiped clean. The theological term is *propitiation*. A word describing the payment that satisfies the wrath of God, which He requires because He is just. But even in justice, He is merciful and doesn't stop there. He knows we can't fix our mess any more than the criminal hanging next to His Son. So because He is merciful beyond measure, He makes the payment on our behalf. Making Him both just and justifier.[5]

This is the mystery, the majesty, the I-just-can't-wrap-my-head-around-it wonder of the cross.

Consider the inconceivability of that. God, who made you, me, the Milky Way, and the hippopotamus, sent His only, perfect, and beloved Son on a rescue mission, a prisoner swap, Him for us. And it's not like we're model citizens. We're all just a bunch of wretched, black-hearted rebels, hell-bent on mutiny. Despite this, His sinless Son lays down His life for us and makes payment for our sin. Why? Jesus answers this just before He goes to the cross. He's talking with His Father: "That the love with which You loved Me may be in them, and I in them."[6] The reason for Jesus is to return us to the arms of the Father so that we might be loved by Him.

What kind of King does this?

I write words for a living, but I have none for this. My response is to fall on my face, surrender wholeheartedly, and cry out, "Lord, have mercy. Remember me when You come into Your kingdom."

Throughout Scripture every time someone saw Jesus in His glorified self, they fell on their faces as though dead. Isaiah saw Jesus, fell on his face, and said, "I am undone. I am unclean." Job lost everything. Family. Wealth. Health. Sitting in boils listening to his "friends" rake God over the coals. Then God shows up. They have a conversation. Job's response? "I know that You can do everything, and that no purpose of Yours can be withheld from You. . . . I have heard of You by the hearing of the ear, but now my eye sees You. Therefore I abhor myself, and repent in dust and ashes."[7]

Saul was a bloodthirsty, state-sponsored terrorist, murdering Christians. On a hunting trip for more heads. But then he bumps into Jesus, and Saul becomes Paul.

Point being, when we see Jesus for who He is, we are changed. Forever.

What you hold is a compilation of stories I wrote and put together in two longer books titled *What If It's True?* and *They Turned the World Upside Down.* I hope you read them, but I wanted to also offer you a singular canvas. In this book I am simply lifting up Jesus. At least, I hope it's simple.

One note for those of you who are smarter than me or know Scripture better than I do: Do I know for certain that everything I say in these stories is exactly right? No. In my defense, I've attempted to use Scripture to interpret the Bible, and I am well aware of that admonition in Revelation that it is really bad for anyone who adds anything to Scripture. By gifting and profession, I am a storyteller. It's what I do. I am offering this book in the same way that writers who came before me, like Lewis, Tolkien, Percy, and MacDonald, have attempted to use story to tell the gospel. Percy called them *"road signs to Jerusalem."* Am I comparing myself to these giants? No. Saint Bernard of Clairvaux wrote what he called the doctrine of Christian humility. In it he said we are all but dwarfs perched atop the shoulders of giants. I'm just a very small writer, and these are my giants.

Let me end with this: The prophet Daniel had a vision that he had trouble explaining. It's well known. Every Hebrew boy would have known it. And what Daniel begins, the apostle John finishes in Revelation. Daniel describes the throne room. The place where God, the Ancient of Days, sits. His clothing is like white snow, hair like pure wool, and His throne is on fire. Continually. There is a river that flows from underneath His throne, and millions upon millions of angels are serving and tending and singing and standing before Him. When God takes His seat, Daniel says, "The books were opened." As a writer, I love the thought that there are books, or scrolls, in heaven. That somehow the written word endures.

That said, these books are a little different. Not the kind you want to read. They record every deed ever committed by us. Either good or bad. These books are our debt ledger. They record every time we sinned against the Ancient of Days. The sum of what we owe. And it's more than we can ever repay. What's more, God is not indifferent to the words in those books. The total record of our sin. He hates it. His wrath is stored up against it. He won't simply overlook it. Won't brush it under the rug.

With court in session, Daniel continues looking. The boastful beast is slain, its body destroyed, thrown into the fire, and the rest of the beasts are reduced to nothing. But that doesn't clear the debt. Payment has to be made. The books are still open. How will the sin of all mankind be atoned for? Paid for? Who is worthy to clear the slate?

Remember when John the Baptist said, "Behold! The Lamb of God who takes away the sin of the world!"?[8] This is the moment that happens.

As Daniel watches, the clouds part: "One like a son of man . . . came to the Ancient of Days and was presented before him."[9] We don't know what was said because Daniel can't hear that. I tend to think Jesus presented His wounds, the holes, His stripes, then poured out every last drop of His blood and said, "*Tetelestai*," but that's just a guess. Whatever is done and said, the Father accepts the Son's payment. In full. Before Daniel's very eyes, the blood of Jesus wipes the slate clean for everyone who believes in—trusts in—the Son. This is why the apostle John said, "The blood of Jesus Christ . . . cleanses us from all sin."[10] In recognition of the Son's perfect sacrifice, God gives His Son "dominion and glory and a kingdom, that all peoples, nations, and languages should serve Him. His dominion is an everlasting dominion, which shall not pass away, and His kingdom the one which shall not be destroyed."[11]

Jesus uses the title Son of Man to refer to Himself almost eighty times in the Gospels, and every time He does, He is referencing this moment. Driving a stake in this earth and in the ears of the kingdom of darkness and saying, "I am the Son of God. I am ransoming mankind with My blood. I am returning to My Father, and I am taking a host with Me." The religious rulers of the day killed Jesus because He claimed to be the Son of God, but His claim is even stronger than that. By calling Himself Son of Man, He is saying, "I am the fulfillment of Daniel's vision, presented before the throne and accepted by the Father. All rule and authority and dominion is given to Me. And My kingdom is never ending."

Were it not true, it would be the most ridiculous claim in all of history.

This book, *Son of Man*, is my attempt to lift up Jesus and add my name to the millions of saints who've come before me, agreeing with Jesus' own statement. He is who He says He is. The only begotten Son of God. For reasons I'll not soon understand, He loves us with a love I just can't fathom. He left His throne, came here on a rescue mission, and died my death. Paid my debt. Wiped my slate. But He doesn't leave me floating in the ether, tending to myself. He wraps me in His arms and brings me to His Father. Which shreds me because I know me, and I'm so unworthy. I don't belong. And yet here I am. I'm at a loss.

This is the unmerited grace of the Ancient of Days.

Writing this, tears stream my face. I can't wrap my head around a King who would do that for me. And for you. And yet He did. He does. Proof there is more grace in Jesus than sin in us.

I can't prove it, but I think our thief on the cross comes to understand this. By the grace of God, the light clicks on, the veil disappears, and He *sees* Jesus. Lifted up. And that revelation turns his heart inside out. When it does, he can't bow, can't lift his hands, can't do anything about anything. All he can do is speak, "Please remember me."

And in beautiful grace-filled fashion, Jesus does.

What kind of King . . .

PRAY WITH ME: *Lord Jesus, I bring You this reader. You know them better than they know themselves because You made them. Fashioned them. You know every wrinkle. Every spot. Every hair. And You've been waiting for this moment. I pray that right now You would visit them with Your salvation. I know Your arm is not so short that it cannot save, and that You uphold all things by the word of Your power, so will You please hold this man, this woman, this child, this adulterer, this prodigal, this liar, this prisoner, this thief, this criminal, this murderer, this rebel, in the palm of Your hand, and will You please remove the veil. Please, Lord, take it away. Your word says that while we were dead, You made us alive. Please, Lord, do what only You can do, and make them alive. Right now. Let us see ourselves in light of You. Like the criminal on the cross, give us a right revelation of who You are. The One who took all our sin and shame and the consequences of all our rebellion and died in our place. Show us what You showed the criminal who hung next to You. Give us a front-row seat. To You. To the blood dripping off Your toes. To the mercy pouring out Your lips. God Most High, please use this road sign to point us to You and give us a right revelation of Your Son, the Man on the middle cross. Because when we see Jesus, Your kindness leads us to repentance. And where there is repentance, these words*

ring out: "Truly you will be with Me today in paradise."
I pray this in the matchless, magnificent, undefeated, and
grace-filled name of Jesus—Son of God and Son of Man.
Amen.

ENTERING THE COURTROOM

I enter the courtroom. Bound. Chains rattling. All eyes on me. Leading up to the trial, the headlines declared me "the Worst of the Worst." The bailiff seats me behind bulletproof glass as the King enters. All rise, save me. Why would I rise? He's about to kill me. The King takes His seat, and with His permission, the proceedings begin. The judge asks me how I plead. I mutter with smug indifference, "Not guilty." While I'm at it, I give the King the finger.

The prosecution brings out a book. Actually, several books. The record of my wrongs. Starting at the beginning, he details my life's work. The list is long but, in short, I am a rebel who committed treason, led a mutiny, and willingly aided and abetted the enemy. All in an attempt to overthrow the King. The beloved King seated above me.

Moans and murmurs bubble up out of the public seats. Midway through the reading, the prosecution lowers an IMAX screen, clicks a button, and begins playing the video of my life's work. The first few images are met with silence but are soon followed by screams, tears, and finally cries for justice. Off to my left, someone vomits. The courtroom is in an uproar. The judge slams his gavel and demands silence. The King wipes away either tears or sweat. The prosecution continues.

For days.

By week's end, the galley is enraged and foaming at the mouth. Several members of the public have been arrested trying to bring weapons into the courtroom. The King sits cross-legged, tapping His fingers, eyes trained on me. Someone leaks a copy of the video to the media. In minutes, the demonstration outside the courthouse turns violent. Armed troops are called in to prevent protesters from storming the courthouse. Fires and looting spread for blocks. Their chants echo through the windows.

They are calling for my head on a platter.

Back inside, we continue to watch the video of me. Murder. Mayhem. Chaos. Adultery. Every drug known to man. Catastrophic theft. Insurrection. School bombings. Playgrounds littered with parts. Assassination attempt after assassination attempt on the life of the King. The video paints a timeline strewn with bodies and people and hopes and dreams, and framing it all is my smiling, grinning, smug little face.

I did what I wanted, when I wanted, how I wanted, whenever I wanted, and I asked no one's permission. I lived for me. Period. Finally, the video displayed one of my mountain homes where the view stretched for miles. Epic parties. Filth untold. In the great room, I'd installed a replica of the King's throne. Surrounded with half-dressed and undressed women. Sex slaves at my beck and call. Minions. The video continued showing me, sitting on the throne, stabbing a life-sized doll of the King. Mutilating Him. In the last frame, I cut off His head and pose for the camera.

Back in the courtroom, there's little deliberation.

The jury files in and the bailiff makes me stand as the judge takes his seat. The verdict is read. Guilty on all counts. The King again wipes either tears or sweat. The judge asks me if I have anything to say. For the second time, I give him the finger. The time for talking is over. The time for dying has arrived. The judge slams the gavel, "Death by firing squad." The bailiff wastes no time. He walks me to a holding cell and strips me to my underwear. My tattered clothes lie in a pile. The smell curls his nose. I'm not much to look at. He then leads me to the yard. Dead man walking. Straps me to a pole. Beyond the bars of the prison, the city is shouting. Screaming for blood. They press against the gates. Testing the locks. The troops wrestle to hold them back. It's not long now. I stare at the rifles all staring at me. I wonder how it will feel when the bullets tear at my flesh and rip off my face. Will I feel anything? Even now, I can feel the heat of my destination rising up around my feet.

I look around for the last time, and one thing strikes me. I am alone. Utterly and completely. Not one single friend can be found. The bailiff speaks to the riflemen, "Ready!" They level them at me. I could stick my finger in the end of the barrels. "Aim!" The rifles steady. At least it will be quick.

One second. Two. Their knuckles turn white as they place pressure on the triggers.

A voice speaks quietly to my left. He's calm. Collected. "Stop." The barrels lift and we turn. The King has appeared. Walking toward me. He's young. Beloved. Beaming. The crowd cheers. Women faint. Children dance. He stands before me. Studies me. I read His face, and despite my every attempt to end His life, I see no anger there. Only sadness. Tears streak His cheeks. With little notice, He takes off His robe and hands it to an attendant. Followed by the ring on His hand. As He does this, I am struck by the knowledge that He is wearing my clothes. My soiled rags.

These are no clothes for a King.

He steps closer. His face inches from mine. His breath on my face. I can smell Him. I am waiting for the condemnation. The words I deserve. Then He does the strangest thing. He kisses me and then whispers through a smile,

"You are . . . the joy set before me." The bailiff unties my ropes, and the King places a thick envelope in my hands. When He turns to face the rifles, the bailiff lashes Him with my ropes to the pole, steps back, and shouts, "Fire!"

Bullets tear at His flesh and almost rip His head off His shoulders. The shockwave slams Him against the pole, then drops Him, limp and bullet-riddled, to the ground. Eyes still open. The life that was there seconds ago is gone. His blood collects into a pool and seeps into the grass. Warm and red. And as it does, I can hear it crying out from the ground.

The crowd disperses, and I am left alone with the body of the dead King.

That night, I stand at the window of a high-rise building. I'm dressed in a brilliant white linen shirt. Unstained. It smells like the King, and I'm pretty sure I shouldn't be wearing it. The carpet is soft beneath my bare feet, and I am not repulsed at the smell of me.

I look over my shoulder because I know me, and I don't belong here. Any minute, armed men will walk through that door and escort me back to the pole where they will finish their count. I study the streets below, but there are no crowds.

Minutes pass, but there are no footsteps. The silence is deafening.

I press my face to the glass, stare out across the world laid out below me, and I can see for more than a hundred miles in every direction. Nothing about my present situation makes sense. The unopened envelope sits on the table next to me. My hand shakes as I open the envelope, revealing a hand-written letter followed by several legal documents.

The letter begins "Dear Son—" and the handwriting belongs to the King, but I can't wrap my head around it. It can't possibly be true. So I read it again. There must be some mistake. Then a third time. I can't figure out who He's talking to. I stare out the window. According to the letter, I now own the building I am standing in and every building for miles in every direction. Further, I own the land, every house, and every beast for more than a hundred miles in all directions. I keep reading, but it is the next revelation that brings me to my knees. A birth certificate. Mine. Yellowed from age.

The date of the letter catches my eye. Someone has made a colossal mistake. I turn to page one of my arrest record—the books they read in court—and the letter predates my first conviction. I empty the remaining contents of the envelope to find a thick stack of accounting spreadsheets. A debt ledger. Mine. I flip through it. Debits and very few credits. The ones I accrued over my wasted life. The last time I looked at my balance due, it was a number I couldn't pay in a hundred lifetimes. When I flip to the last page, afraid of what I know I owe, I am awestruck.

A zero balance.

The knowledge swims around my head, and the enormity of it settles somewhere in my heart—the King filed the adoption papers while I was busy writing my book. Accruing insurmountable debt. While I was trying to kill Him and grab His power. My strength fails, I hit my knees, and somewhere in that fog, my heart is pierced with the knowingness that He didn't disown me when He had every right. When He could have. What's more, He didn't shame me. When He should have. What I am holding in my hand, if it is true, tells me that the King paid all my debts, served my sentence, and gave me all He had.

He made me His own.

A noise behind me. An older man. Beard. He resembles the King. His scent is somehow familiar. The picture on the desk suggests they are related. Father and Son. I peer around Him, but there are no armed guards. His face is not threatening. He steps closer. His breath on my face. I hold up the documents. "Is this true?"

A tear breaks loose. A smile. And He nods. "Every word."

I point to the books, stacked in the corner. The ones used by the prosecution. "But—" I stammer. "I'm guilty. Don't you realize? I did all this. Every last thing." I point to the picture of the Son. "And He didn't do a thing." I shake my head. "You killed the wrong man."

He says nothing.

I scream, "But why?!"

The Father wraps His arms around me, and that's when it hits me. He sent His Son. To rescue me. To do for me what I could not do for myself. When I wasn't worth rescuing.

I am undone.

GOD WITH US

They are arranged in laser-perfect rows. Ten thousand in a row and tens of thousands of rows. Trailing out farther than any eye can see. They are radiant and barefooted. Every shade of skin color dressed in a sea of brilliant white robes. Decked in glistening gold. Chiseled, elegant features. Blond, auburn, ebony hair. The floor on which they are dancing is reflective. Shiny. Not a speck. Not a smudge. They stand somewhere above ten feet tall. Many have hair to their waists. Some pulled back in a ponytail. Their wings stretch another ten feet into the air, the tips are almost touching. They are frozen in time, holding the same choreographed pose each was holding when the music stopped. Along with everyone else, they are waiting for the music to begin again and send them into the next movement. Right now, they are catching their breath and waiting for orders. Heads bowed, beads of sweat drip onto the mirrored floor.

The air carries with it the fading echo of a drumbeat and the receding sound of the concert of a million feet dancing and tapping to perfection. It's a powerful, penetrating rhythm felt in the depths. Several miles in the distance, there is a bright light. Brighter than the sun. It is the most piercing and penetrating light in the history of light. The breeze created by the angels' wings brings with it the smell of mint, rosemary, lavender, lemon, and eucalyptus. This place is an architectural wonder. Planes could fly in here. A thousand planes. A river flows through the middle. A roof above. In the distance, fiery stones.

This is the banquet hall of all banquet halls.

Rising on the air is a chorus of voices. They come from higher up. Thundering. Declaring. Proclaiming. Pitch perfect. While each is distinct, they layer over each other. The melody forms and rises. They are reading from an ancient text. The acoustics are perfect and unamplified.

The first voice speaks of how He will be born of a woman. Another states that He will come from the line of Abraham. Another, the tribe of Judah. The house of David. Born of a virgin. Will sit on the throne of David. An eternal throne. Emmanuel. Born in Bethlehem. Worshiped by wise men. Presented with gifts. Called out of Egypt. Called a Nazarene.

The voices continue—He will be zealous for His Father. Filled with God's Spirit. Heal many. Deal gently with Gentiles. Rejected by His own. Speak in parables. Enter triumphantly into Jerusalem. Praised by little children. A cornerstone. Perform miracles—which some would not believe. Betrayed for thirty pieces of silver that would be used to buy a potter's field. A man of sorrows. Acquainted with grief. Forsaken by His own best friends. Scourged. Spat on. Unrecognizable as a man. Crucified between two thieves. Given vinegar to drink. His hands and feet would be pierced. Others would gamble for and divide His clothes. Surrounded and ridiculed by His enemies. He would thirst, commend His spirit to His Father, and not one of His bones would be broken. Stared at in death, buried with the rich, raised from the dead, He would ascend and become a greater high priest than Aaron. He would rule the heathen. A ruling scepter. Seated at the right hand of God.

As the last word echoes off, all eyes turn toward the light several miles in the distance where a King is seated on His throne. He is resplendent. Like ten thousand nuclear bombs exploding over and over and over. He is magnificent. Splendor indescribable. Majesty on high. *El Elyon.* The brightness of the sun times ten trillion. To His right sits His Son. The very Word of God. Broad shoulders, the spitting image. A river—crystal clear—flows from beneath His throne. In His hand, He holds a scepter. He is radiant.

Nothing has been, is, or ever will be more perfect. He is like a jasper stone and a sardius in appearance, and there is a rainbow wrapped around His throne like an emerald. From the throne come flashes of lightning and peals of thunder.[1]

Layered in the air, the several-million-voice chorus rises: "Glory to God in the highest!" The shimmering, angelic bodies below snap into unison. Twirling. Tapping. Synchronized. Each dancer has six wings. Two cover their faces. Two cover their feet. And with two more they fly. Cirque du Soleil doesn't hold a candle.

Voices sing out: "Only begotten Son."[2]

"Heir of all things, through whom He also made the world. And He is the radiance of His glory and the exact representation of His nature, and upholds all things by the word of His power."[3]

"For by Him all things were created, both in the heavens and on earth . . . whether thrones, or dominions, or rulers, or authorities—all things have been created through Him and for Him. He is before all things, and in Him all things hold together."[4]

"He who is the blessed and only Sovereign, the King of kings and Lord of lords, who alone possesses immortality and dwells in unapproachable light, whom no one has seen or can see. To Him be honor and eternal dominion!"[5]

"He was in the beginning with God. All things were made through Him, and without Him nothing was made that was made. In Him was life, and the life was the light of men. And the light shines in the darkness, and the darkness did not comprehend it."[6]

"The Alpha and the Omega . . . who is and who was and who is to come, the Almighty."[7]

"The Amen, the Faithful and True Witness, the Beginning of the creation of God."[8]

"The Lion that is from the tribe of Judah, the Root of David."[9]

Then the voices hush. Every angel kneels. Bowing. Face to the floor. Twenty-four elders, each holding a harp and a bowl of incense—which are the prayers of the saints—lie on the ground in a circle around Him, having cast their crowns at His feet.

The Son is quiet. Unassuming. No desire to draw attention. Not feeling that equality with the King is something to be grasped. His mannerisms are that of a dove. His presence that of a lion. His demeanor like a lamb's. His attraction like the bright morning star. Expressing both longing and joy. Both tears and a smile.

He is attended by an archangel. One of three. This angel is relatively new at his job. The other two have been here a long time. The last archangel who had attended to Jesus was described as the "seal of perfection, full of wisdom and perfect in beauty."[10] He announced the morning but eventually grew jealous of all the praise leveled at the Son. Wanting it, he reached up, tried to grab it, and fell. Disguising himself as an angel of light, he led a rebellion, and he took a third of the other angels with him. Mutiny. God the Father would have none of it and cast the dark angel out of heaven like lightning. Hurling him earthward where he has stirred up trouble for millennia.

After he left, the King made a new creation out of dust. His most stunning to date. Made in His very image. When finished, the King pressed His lips to the mouth of His creation and breathed in His very breath. The *ruach* of God. Giving man life. Angry and envious, the rebelling angel slithered in and took them all hostage. Kidnapped everyone. Bondage. Slavery. Mass carnage.

Things are bad. The only hope is a rescue mission. It's why the Son has to leave. Whispers are it's a suicide mission.

Slowly, the Son rises. It is pin-drop quiet. He places His scepter gently in the corner of His throne. Unbuckling His sword, he leans it upright next to the scepter. Next, He takes off His robe, folds it, and places it in the seat He just occupied. He pulls off His tasseled linen undershirt and places it neatly next to His robe, folding the corners gently. Finally, He removes the ring from His finger and lifts His crown off His brow, placing both atop His folded robe.

Save a loincloth, the Son stands naked. His voice is the sound of many waters. Like Niagara. Or the break at Pipeline.

God the Father rises as His Son crosses the fiery stones. The Father hugs the Son, buries His face in His Son's cheek, and kisses Him. The time has come. On earth, the sons of Adam have lost their way. Each gone their own way. Astray. The entire human race has been taken captive, and the enemy is torturing them. Not one of them will survive the night. The Son has volunteered for a rescue mission, but it's a prisoner exchange. The whispers are true; their freedom will cost the Son everything. His life for theirs.

The Father holds His Son's hands in His and tenderly touches the center of His palm. He knows what's coming. A tear rolls down the face of the Ancient of Days. The Son thumbs it away. "I'll miss you." He glances at the earth below and hell in between. Billions of faces shine across the timeline of history. He knows each by name. They are the "joy set before Him."[11] He turns to His Father. "I will give them Your word. And declare to them Your great name."[12] The Son looks with longing at His home.

Voices rise from every corner, everyone singing at the top of their lungs. It is the loudest singing in the history of song. "Blessing and honor and glory and power be to Him who sits on the throne, and to the Lamb, forever and ever!"[13] Angels bow. Brush the floor. He pats many on the shoulder. Kisses some. Hugs others. Long-held embraces. Kids rush forward and grab His hands as they dance in laughter-filled circles.

As He turns to leave, leaning against the two giant doors that lead out into the Milky Way, He turns to His Father. His eyes are piercing, penetrating, inviting. He smiles. "We're going to need more rooms in this house when I come back." He waves His hand across the timeline. "Because I'm bringing them with Me." The Son—whose countenance is "like the sun shining in its strength"[14]—exits heaven blanketed in the singing of more than a hundred million angels and bathed in the tears of the Father.

The Word becomes flesh, and He is gone.

In the beginning was the Word, and the Word was with God, and the Word was God. He was in the beginning with God. . . . And the Word became flesh and dwelt among us, and we beheld His glory.[15]

———— ⊫⬦⊨ ————

About nine months later . . .

The night is cool and turning cooler. The air smells of wood smoke, lamp oil, and manure. Quirinius is governing Syria. Caesar Augustus has issued a decree: "Register the world! Take a census." Under the dominating hand of Rome, men and their families scurry to their ancestral homes to register. Jerusalem is overflowing. Bethlehem is packed.

It is dark. Past the evening meal. A young man leads a

young girl riding a donkey up a small trail into Bethlehem. He is pensive. Every few seconds, he glances over his shoulder.

The rumors have preceded them. As have the whispers. She's pregnant but not with his child, and to complicate matters, they're not married. It's a scandal. According to Jewish law, he should put her out, and she should be stoned.

The innkeeper has had a long day. He watches warily. The tired young man asks, "Sir, do you have a room?"

The innkeeper shakes his head. "Full up."

The young man strains his voice. "You know of . . . anywhere?"

The innkeeper leans on his broom handle. Half-annoyed. His patience is thin. "Try down there. But you're wasting your time."

The girl winces. The contractions have started. The stain on her dress suggests her water broke. The innkeeper's wife eyes the barn and whispers, "We can make room."

<hr />

Hours pass, and the couple returns. The young girl is sweating. Doubled over. The young man is frantic. The innkeeper is in bed. Upon hearing the knock, he rises reluctantly and unlocks the door. "Son, I told you . . ."

"Please, sir . . ." He points to the young woman. "She's bleeding."

The innkeeper's wife appears over his shoulder. She says nothing, which says plenty. The innkeeper trims his wick and, for the first time, looks into the young man's eyes. The innkeeper gently grabs the reins of the donkey and leads the young woman to the barn, where he spreads fresh hay to make a bed. His wife appears with a towel and some rags. She brushes the two men out and helps the girl.

The innkeeper and the young man stand at the door of the stable—little more than a cave carved into the rock wall. The animals seem amused at the ruckus. The innkeeper lights his pipe. The young man shuffles nervously.

Behind them, the screams begin.

The innkeeper speaks first. "You the two everyone is talking about?"

The young man doesn't take his eyes off the cave. "Yes, sir."

Another puff. Another cloud. "What happened?"

The young man is not quick to answer. "You wouldn't believe me if I told you."

The innkeeper laughs, "I don't know. I was young once. She's a pretty girl."

Another scream echoes out of the barn.

"Is the baby yours?"

The young man rubs his hands together. Calloused, muscled. They are the hands of a stonemason. "No, He's not. I mean, He will be, but . . . I'm not the, well . . ."

The innkeeper chuckles. "You sure it's a he?"

The young man nods. "Pretty sure."

"You intend to marry?"

The young man glances over his shoulder. "Soon as she heals up."

Another scream and the innkeeper changes the subject. "You here to register?"

The young man nods.

"What family?"

"House of David."

The innkeeper raises an eyebrow. "Good family."

The screams have risen to a fever pitch. The young girl is out of her mind. The innkeeper's wife calls from the stall. Her voice trembles. "Honey, I need some hot water."

The innkeeper disappears and leaves the young man alone. He stands repeating the same phrase over and over and over. "Hear, O Israel: the LORD our God, the LORD is one! Hear, O Israel . . ."[16]

Above, a star has risen. Abnormally bright.

—⋅—⋈⋛⋈—⋅—

A short time later, the innkeeper returns as the cries of a baby pierce the night air. The child's lungs are strong. The wife clears the mucus, and the cries grow louder. The young man exhales a breath he has been holding for a little over nine months. The innkeeper stokes the fire in the corner and hugs the young man. "Come!"

The hay beneath the young woman is a mess. The baby boy has entered the world in much the same way the nation of Israel left Egypt. Through blood and water. The animals look on. The stones cry out.[17]

The woman places the baby on the mother's chest, and the two lie exhausted. The young woman is exposed, and the young man is uncertain as to his role. He has yet to know her. The innkeeper's wife leads him to the young girl's side, where he cuts the cord and then slides his hand inside hers. His heart is racing. She is exhausted. Sweaty. The afterbirth arrives, and the innkeeper's wife begins cleaning the woman. The young mother stares at the boy and hears the echo of the angel that appeared to her some ten months ago: "He will be great, and will be called the Son of the Highest; and the Lord God will give Him the throne of His father David. And He will reign over the house of Jacob forever, and of His kingdom there will be no end."[18]

This is a bittersweet moment because she knows well the words of both Isaiah and the psalmist. How the Messiah will suffer. Be cursed. Bruised. Pierced. Despised. Rejected. Oppressed. Afflicted. Cut off from the land of the living. He will bear our griefs. Carry our sorrows. All His bones will be out of joint. His heart will melt like wax. He will give His back to those who will beat Him, pour out His soul unto death, bear the sin of many . . . and become unrecognizable as a man.[19]

She turns to the man who did not leave her when he had every right. The honorable man who will be her husband. She hands him the boy and speaks His name, "*Yeshua Hamashiach.*"

The young father holds his son and whispers, "The Sun of Righteousness shall arise with healing in His wings."[20]

The innkeeper and his wife stand at a distance. They can't take their eyes off the boy. She whispers, "Every male who opens the womb shall be called holy to the LORD."[21] On the air above them there is an echo. Faint at first, it grows louder. The innkeeper stares at heaven. The star above them is daylight bright and casts their shadows on the ground. Finally, he can make it out. Voices. Purest he's ever heard. Singing at the top of their lungs: "Glory to God in the highest, and on earth peace, goodwill toward men!"[22]

The innkeeper knows now. He bows low and speaks loud enough for the young couple to hear: "The Lord Himself will give you a sign: Behold, the virgin shall conceive and bear a Son, and shall call His name Immanuel."[23]

God with us.

But not all are so inviting. In the dark night air, invisible armies draw invisible battle lines. Forces gather. Battle plans are drawn. Even now, the boy's life is in danger.

Just over the next hill, beyond earshot, lies another hill.

Mount Moriah. It is an ancient and storied place. It is the hill where Melchizedek reigned as priest to God Most High. Where Abraham raised the knife above Isaac. The hill where Ornan the Jebusite built his threshing floor. Where the plague stopped. Where David danced before the Lord and returned the ark. The hill where Solomon built the temple. And in about three decades, forces will gather on this hill to execute this boy.

Daylight breaks the horizon, the innkeeper tends the fire. "The people who walked in darkness have seen a great light; those who dwelt in the land of the shadow of death, upon them a light has shined."[24] Mary wraps Jesus tightly in swaddling clothes, lifts Him from the stone trough, and cradles the suckling baby, "who, being in the form of God, did not consider it robbery to be equal with God, but made Himself of no reputation, taking the form of a bondservant, and coming in the likeness of men. And being found in appearance as a man, He humbled Himself and became obedient."[25]

Joseph kneels and presses his lips to the forehead of his son. He knows the words by heart. Written 740 years ago, Isaiah was speaking about his son. About this very moment. About this improbable beginning. About this King who stepped off His throne to become a boy who will grow into a man and walk from this cave to that hill—and down into hell—to ransom many.

For unto us a Child is born,
Unto us a Son is given;
And the government will be upon His
     shoulder.
And His name will be called
Wonderful, Counselor, Mighty God,
Everlasting Father, Prince of Peace.
Of the increase of His government and peace
There will be no end,
Upon the throne of David and over His
     kingdom,
To order it and establish it with judgment and
     justice
From that time forward, even forever.
The zeal of the LORD of hosts will perform
     this.[26]

DAUGHTER OF GOD

J esus steps out of the boat, and the crowds rush the beach. The country of the Gadarenes sits behind Him. Across the water. The rumors have already spread. A man tormented by demons is now in his right mind, and a herd of pigs is drowned.[1]

His disciples are whispering. One of them thumbs over his back. "Did you see that?"

Another nods. "Yeah, I saw it, but I don't know what to do with it."

A third speaks. "I've never even thought something like that."

Jesus laughs. He has several appointments to keep. What happens in these next few minutes will upend the world.

A man runs across the beach. Robes flowing. He's wealthy. One of the rulers of the synagogue. He darts through the crowd. The apostles move to protect Jesus when Jairus falls at His feet and begs Him earnestly. "My little daughter lies at the point of death. Come and lay Your hands on her, that she may be healed, and she will live."[2]

Jesus smiles and gestures with His hand. "Take Me to her."

Moving through the street, Jairus screams at the crowd, fearing his daughter's death, "Move!" But Jesus is not hurried. In fact, He slows. Purposefully.

He chose this street. He has been waiting for this day. This moment. The crowd squeezes in, but He's not bothered. He is taking His time. He catches a glimpse of her behind Him, and His heart leaps. He knows her by name. There she is again. Weaving through the crowd, desperation painted across her face. He is her last hope, and He knows it. He smiles to Himself.

She's heard the stories. Word has spread throughout all Judea. There was the man with the withered hand. The centurion's servant. The son of the widow of Nain who was in a coffin being carried out through the gate. The paralyzed man lowered by his friends through a roof who, after the Healer touched him, walked out the front door. How He calmed the wind and the waves with just a word. How He laid His hands on those with various diseases and how He healed them all. Every one. Lastly, she's heard how He delivered the demon-possessed man of the Gadarenes. And then, just recently, she's heard how He read the prophet Isaiah in the synagogue. How the Spirit of the Sovereign Lord was upon Him. She knew the prophecy.

He is the Healer. The One the prophets talked about.

Through no fault of her own, she'd been bleeding for twelve years.[3] Everything that she touched, lay down on, sat on, or wore—and everything that touched any of these things that she touched, lay down on, sat on, or wore—was unclean. This included people. That meant whoever she touched was unclean.[4] She was not allowed to "be with" a man or for a man to know her. The message given, the law applied to her, was "Stay away. You are cast out." Given her condition, she was excluded from worship and from offering sacrifice—not allowed in the front door. And had been for over a decade. She could not get access to the priest, and, hence, God. There was no atonement. No forgiveness. She didn't shake hands in public. She didn't kiss anyone. Didn't hug anyone. Kept at arm's length.

How many times had she wondered if she'd be better off dead?

Then there was the issue of constantly having to wear a diaper. Something to soak up the blood so it didn't trickle down her leg, but sometimes it soaked through. Sometimes she left a trail. Her shame had soaked through too. In the back of her house, where she dried her laundry, she hung the stained rags. Her neighbors couldn't help but notice when they flapped in the breeze. They wished she'd do something about the smell.

She'd tried everything. Been to every doctor. Now broke, she'd traveled far and spent every penny. The problem had not improved. Only gotten worse.

Everyone knew about her condition, which also meant they knew the source of her shame. It was sin. Either hers or her family's sin had brought this curse on her. The Law of Moses said so. So she lived under the constant shadow of whispers. Whatever sin she'd committed must have been significant. She's paying the penalty. And only God knows why.

Catching a glimpse of Him, something in her stirs. Hope? Desperation? A mixture of both. Being unclean, she cannot get to where He is. They won't let her. The law prohibits it. She knows she is not allowed around other people. She's been forced to live and sustain herself on the outskirts, and—if she knows anything at all—she is certainly not allowed to reach out and touch anyone. Most of all Him. But she doesn't care what they think.

She has come to the end of herself.

She doubles the cloth rag between her legs. Covers her head more so than usual, crowding her eyes and brow so that she might not be recognized. The crowd passes. He is in the middle. Everyone's attention is focused on Him. She files in behind. Out of sight. Then, gathering her nerve, she begins picking up her step, working closer. Weaving.

Elbowing. If she is caught, she will be disciplined. Greater shame. Complete and total public embarrassment. Both bleeder and believer, she picks her way through the crowd.

Just a few steps away, the crowd encroaches. She has to elbow her way through. She knows she is in violation. If she's caught—she doesn't want to think about it. A few more steps and there He is. An arm's length. Standing next to Him are several men who look like they are from Galilee. The big, loud one must be Peter. She's heard of him too. The crowd shoves, and pushes, and tightens, and she is losing sight of this Man named Jesus of Nazareth. In desperation, she lunges, extends her reach, and grasps the corner of His garment. His shirt. The tassel. The wing. She clings. Holds tightly.

He feels the tug. Feels the power leave.

She feels it enter. Right then and there, her broken body is healed—and she knows it. Twelve years of pain and shame and anger and exasperation begin working their way out of her soul. The tears begin to fall. She tries to back away. To escape. She is trembling. She is shattered. Her knees buckle.

Jesus pauses. Stops. She is fearful of what He might say next. Then He says it. "Who just touched Me?" She is discovered. Found out. More shame. Cast farther out. Will they stone her for so great a violation? Jesus raises His voice. "Who touched Me?" His friends, led by Peter, say, "Master, all these people? Everybody is touching You."

Jesus shakes His head. They don't get it. He is the Sun who has come with healing in His wings,[5] and somebody who both knew and believed that touched Him with intention. The Sun of Righteousness wants her brought before Him. Why? Because He fashioned her. Knit her together. He's known her pain. Has suffered with her. He saw her coming through the crowd. He knows she's been weakened by twelve years of chronic anemia, so He slowed just enough so she could reach out and touch Him. He's not finished with her. Not by a long shot.

He lifts a hand. "Somebody touched Me with intention. Power left My body." Everybody, all those big men, begin looking for the perpetrator in the crowd. The thief.

Trembling, having lost total control of her emotions, pleading on the inside that God would either have mercy on her in this moment or just strike her down, she falls to her knees. Soaks the earth with her tears. Bowing her head, hiding her eyes, she spills it. Lays it out there for the whole world to hear.

"Here is my shame!"

Her cries echo off the stone city walls. She is a woman undone. Laid bare.

Jesus, who knows her name, steps forward. He is so glad to see her. He has missed her, and He has been looking forward to this moment for a long time. He chose this road because He knew it wound near her house. Because while her body is battered and torn, it's her heart that is broken. In this moment, Jesus has already healed her body. The fountain of her blood was already dried up. He is calling her forward because He is about to heal her heart. Then, of all the words He could have spoken, He says the one singular word she needs to hear.

"Daughter."

The word echoes inside her. Dancing around her insides like a pinball until it comes to rest in that place in her gut. Where her soul lives. Down where her hope is buried.

Jesus reaches out and lifts her. Raises her up in front of everyone else. Hugs her. Tightly. While she weeps and smears snot on His shoulder, He welcomes this daughter back into the family. And then just so everybody knows and to ensure there's no doubt, no question, He says, "Your faith has healed you."

Somewhere in there it hits her. "I am healed! It's over. I am what I once was. What I've always longed to be." This knowingness spreads across her face. "I am a child of God!"

ONLY BELIEVE

Standing in the streets of Capernaum, the woman with the issue of blood no longer has the issue. She's healed. Twelve years of shame and rejection are washing themselves out of her heart as she dances her way down the street. Jesus laughs as she twirls. She is a mixture of tears and sobs as she screams at the top of her lungs, "He called me daughter!"

The town is amazed.

The only one not impressed is Jairus, the leader of the synagogue, whose daughter lies at the point of death. He's sweating, hasn't eaten in days, and he's worried. She was hours from death when he left the house and even now it may be too late because Jesus has been messing around with this smelly woman in the street. He got to Him first and yet, for some reason, Jesus held back. Jairus is exasperated. While he's waiting on Jesus to finish with this woman, someone runs from his house. Their face tells the picture. Bad news. His daughter is dead. Don't trouble the teacher any further.

Jesus picks up on their quiet conversation. And Jairus's body language. The shoulder-shaking sob. He knows what they said. He also knows there's no pain like kid pain.

He touches Jairus on the shoulder. "Do not fear; only believe."[1]

Don't fear? Are you kidding me? Jairus is riddled with fear. He's afraid of what he will find when he walks in the door. Afraid of not being able to comfort his wife. Afraid of holding his dead daughter's body. And as for "believe" . . . Believe what? Believe that she's dead? Believe that he never should have left her side? Jairus spits and cusses beneath his breath. He knew he never should have left the house. At least he could have been with her when she passed out of this life.

Dreading what awaits him, Jairus leads the way. Followed by Jesus, Peter, James, and John. The next couple of days for the disciples will be rather action-packed, and Jesus is using this as their training ground.

When they arrive, the house is in turmoil. People are wailing. Loudly. Tearing their clothes. Piling dirt on their heads. Jesus raises a hand, grabs their attention. "The child is not dead, but sleeping."

How insensitive. They laugh Him off. He's lost His mind.

Jesus is tired of both their laughter and what lies beneath it. He puts everyone outside save the father and mother and His three disciples and goes in with the child.

He pokes His head around the corner and smiles. He knows her. He made her. She's twelve, which means she's lived as long as the woman back in the street had the issue of blood. After this, they can share their stories. Compare notes. It's obvious to everyone in the room that she's dead. She looks it. Plus, they heard her breathe her last and she hasn't breathed since. No one can hold their breath that long. Everyone in the house can confirm beyond a shadow of a doubt that Jesus is too late and that the girl is, in fact, dead. It's why they're wailing. And they'd better get busy if they're going to get her buried before sundown.

Jesus kneels next to the bed, pushes the girl's sweaty hair out of her cold, blue, dead face, and then slips His hand inside hers. The mother is clinging to Jairus, who is clinging to his wife. Both are shattered. They thought the teacher could help her. He was their last hope. For who can raise the dead?

Jesus leans forward and speaks softly, as if to wake the girl gently, "Talitha, cumi," which means, "Little girl, I say to you, arise."[2]

In an instant, the girl got up and began walking around.

A dead girl sat up, stepped out of bed, and began walking.

Jesus and His disciples leave the house where a party—shouting, singing, dancing, drinking—has taken the place of a funeral wake. Everyone wants to see the little girl. To touch her. Word spreads like wildfire. She's alive!

IN THE POWER OF JESUS

I t had been a busy and full two days. On the first, Jesus cleansed a leper, healed a centurion's servant, healed Peter's mother-in-law, and, when evening came, He cast demons out of many and healed all who were sick. The following day, needing rest and a break from the crowd, He climbed into a boat with the Twelve and took a nap, only to be awakened a short time later by one of them telling Him how they were all about to die. He rebuked the wind and waves, and all of the disciples for their lack of faith, and then exited the boat in the region of the Gadarenes, where He cast a legion of demons out of a crazed man. With the man now clothed, seated, and in his right mind, Jesus again loaded into the boat and crossed back over to His own city, where they brought Him a paralytic. Jesus forgave his sins, healed him, and the man rose and walked home.

Jesus then called Matthew the tax collector—one of the most hated people in all of society because he'd sold out to Rome—and He ate dinner with him and other tax-gatherers and sinners. Somewhere in all this commotion, one of the synagogue officials came and told Jesus that his daughter was nearly dead. The man pleaded with Him to come and lay hands on his little girl. Jesus turned that direction but slowed in the street to allow a broken and bleeding woman to touch the hem of His garment. When she did, she was healed. The worried father tugged on Jesus' arm. Jesus followed him to his house to find the girl dead and people wailing loudly. Unfazed, Jesus raised the little girl to life and then healed two blind men on His way out of town. While the blind men were still dancing and screaming in the street, Jesus healed another demon-possessed man.

The people begin scratching their heads. "It was never seen like this in Israel!"[1]

And they're right.

The Twelve are watching this with rapt attention. Their heads on swivels.

Until now, the disciples had some context for the miracles Jesus had performed, as miracles were not entirely uncommon in the history of Israel: the dead had been raised to life, leprosy healed, the sun traveled backward, Daniel in the lions' den, Jonah in the belly of the whale, the plagues in Egypt, the Red Sea parting, water from the rock . . .

But there was one miracle for which they had no context: the casting out of demons.

Not only was it new, but it was becoming commonplace in Jesus' ministry.

In their minds they are beginning to think that Jesus can defeat Rome. Usher in a new kingdom right here and now. Stop the oppression. Overturn the tyrant. He possesses a power that they do not. But before the disciples can wrap their heads around what they are seeing with their own eyes, Jesus calls the Twelve together. He is about to do something amazing.

And when He had called His twelve disciples to Him, He gave them power over unclean spirits, to cast them out, and to heal all kinds of sickness and all kinds of disease.[2] "And as you go, preach, saying, 'The kingdom of heaven is at hand.' Heal the sick, cleanse the lepers, raise the dead, cast out demons. Freely you have received, freely give."[3]

The disciples are giddy. Jesus has just done something no king has ever done. He gave them His power. Their minds are racing with possibilities. Unable to contain their excitement, they whisper among themselves. But before they can get too far ahead of themselves, Jesus taps them on the shoulder, brings them in closer—a huddle of sorts—and speaks softly. Saying something they aren't expecting:

Behold, I send you out as sheep in the midst of wolves. Therefore be wise as serpents and harmless as doves. But beware of men, for they will deliver you up to councils and scourge you in their synagogues. You will be brought before governors and kings for My sake, as a testimony to them and to the Gentiles. . . . And you will be hated by all for My name's sake. But he who endures to the end will be saved. . . . And do not fear those who kill the body but cannot kill the soul. But rather fear Him who is able to destroy both soul and body in hell.[4]

The Twelve do as their Master has instructed. "They departed and went through the towns, preaching the gospel and healing everywhere."[5]

So successful are they in their demon-casting-out-and-healing-all-sickness-and-disease campaign that Herod the tetrarch feels threatened. He even starts talking to himself. Questioning himself. "But I beheaded John. Right?" Many thought John the Baptist or Elijah had risen from the dead. The works the disciples are doing are on the level of the greatest ever to carry the name of God.

The disciples return with eyes the size of Oreos. Even they are amazed. They can't believe it. Jesus pulls them away secretly to Bethsaida for a debriefing, but the crowds hear of His presence and start amassing in large numbers. Seeing that it's late, the disciples tell Jesus He'd better send the crowd away. They have a long journey ahead. Jesus, who'd given them all authority and power, says, "You give them something to eat."[6]

A quick inventory reveals five loaves and two fish. A quick head count reveals five thousand men—close to twenty thousand people when wives and children are included.

To their amazement, Jesus feeds the crowd, and they collect twelve baskets of leftover food fragments.

In the days that follow, Peter confesses Jesus as the Christ, Jesus predicts His death and resurrection, and He tells them all that if any wish to follow Him, they must take up their cross. Given that the people haven't yet seen Him crucified, this is a bit of a mystery. It certainly has them puzzled when Jesus is transfigured bright as the sun alongside Moses and Elijah before their very eyes. Not to mention God's very voice echoes out, "This is My beloved Son. Hear Him!"[7] The following day, a father implores Jesus to heal his son, who is constantly thrown into the fire by a demon. Jesus rebukes the demon, heals the child, and hands the boy to his father.

This is the whirlwind in which the disciples find themselves. "And they were all amazed at the majesty of God."[8]

Amazed? These men are out of their minds. They can't believe what they are seeing. Heaven has come to earth. The kingdom of God is at hand.

Eventually, their numbers grow to seventy. Rather than

hoard His power, solidify His position, and grind people beneath His thumb, Jesus shares it—a second time—and empowers others to do the same. Creating coheirs rather than slaves.

Speaking to the seventy, Jesus says, "Go your way; behold, I send you out as lambs among wolves."[9] And after they'd gone and done what He'd told them to do:

> Then the seventy returned with joy, saying, "Lord, even the demons are subject to us in Your name."
>
> And He said to them, "I saw Satan fall like lightning from heaven. Behold, I give you the authority to trample on serpents and scorpions, and over all the power of the enemy, and nothing shall by any means hurt you. Nevertheless do not rejoice in this, that the spirits are subject to you, but rather rejoice because your names are written in heaven."[10]

This is not Jesus the sandal-wearing carpenter speaking. This is Jesus the Bright Morning Star, crown on His head, ring on His finger. He is describing the most awesome battle ever, anywhere. Good versus evil, and good not only drove the enemy back but kicked them out. A complete rout.

Many of the disciples look at their hands, turning them over and back. For in their hands, they now hold that very same power. That casting-satan-down power. There is a gleam on their faces. Fist pumps. Their minds are racing with possibilities. This is just the first huddle before the first play. They are going to run up the score and hand an irrevocable defeat to the enemy.

Forever.

Then comes the cross. Where they stand powerless.

THE GOOD CONFESSION

Jesus has brought them north. Onto the green slopes of the snowcapped peak of Mount Hermon, some twenty-five miles north of the Sea of Galilee. He'd been praying alone at a high place, as was His custom. Now He's brought the disciples to Caesarea Philippi.

The population of Caesarea Philippi is not Jewish, and Jews don't normally come here. They walk around it. The very city was built up and around ancient Syrian temples dedicated to Baal worship. A cave near where the disciples stand is said to be the birthplace of the Greek god Pan, hence the town's original name—Panias. The cave is cut into the side of a high cliff, at the base of which is a crystal-clear spring, which forms the easternmost source of the Jordan River. Stone steps lead to a large, white marble temple that grows out from the side of the cliff. Off to one side sits a large, elaborately carved stone altar several feet tall and several feet square. Large enough to hold human bodies.

The locals call this place "the Gates of Hell." With good reason. Parents sacrifice their children here. A lot. Wishing to please the gods, they throw their babies in a bubbling, rushing spring that soon disappears below earth, allowing them a few seconds to run to the river's next surface appearance some yards distant. If they see red, the gods have rejected the sacrifice. If no red, then they've appeased the gods. Sacrifice accepted.

The altar is stained from human sacrifice and the residue of the sex of temple priests. Along the edges, slave hands have carved a blood groove. Like a moat. Priests capture the blood and drink it as ceremony in their orgies.

To the Hebrews—the children of the promise—this is defiled, unholy, and cursed ground. It's the worst place any of them could imagine standing.

Against this backdrop of idol worship, Jesus asks an amazing question. "Who do men say that I, the Son of Man, am?"[1] This is no small question. In fact, it is *the* question. Subtle voices echo out of the Twelve. "Elijah." "John the Baptist." "Jeremiah." "One of the prophets."

Oddly, the self-appointed spokesperson of the group, Peter, is silent. In fact, Peter is scratching his head. A wrinkle sits between his eyes. He can't for the life of him understand why they are standing where they are standing.

Finally, Jesus turns to him. "Who do you say that I am?"

This time Peter is not silent. He steps forward. "You are the Christ, the Son of the living God."[2]

These are no small words Peter is speaking. They are earth-shattering, stratosphere-rocking, mind-blowing words. Peter, a Jew who could probably recite by memory much of what we would call the first five books of the Bible along with much of the Prophets, Psalms, and Proverbs, is saying that this man Jesus is the answer to more than six hundred Old Testament prophecies regarding the promised Messiah. That He is the long-awaited Christ. The Savior of the world.

These words could get him killed.

Later in his life, they will.

Jesus nods. They are starting to get it.

Jesus answered and said to him, "Blessed are you, Simon Bar-Jonah, for flesh and blood has not revealed this to you, but My Father who is in heaven. And I also say to you that you are Peter, and on this rock I will build My church, and the gates of Hades shall not prevail against it. And I will give you the keys of the kingdom of heaven, and whatever you bind on earth will be bound in heaven, and whatever you loose on earth will be loosed in heaven."[3]

NEITHER DO I CONDEMN YOU

It's early. The sun is just up. Jesus is in the temple. Teaching. People are sitting close. Packed in like sardines.

There's a commotion at the door. Loud voices. Several Pharisees drag in a woman. Caught in the act of sleeping with a man—not her husband. Adultery. The woman is completely naked. The man, mind you, is nowhere to be found.

They throw her down. "We caught her!" They laugh, letting their eyes walk up and down her body. She wraps her arms around her knees, trying to conceal herself with long hair. The scribes continue. One is tossing a stone in the air like a baseball. They are baiting Jesus. Their voices are ripe with cynicism. "Moses commands us to stone her." They have no interest in His answer. Only their trap.

Jesus stoops down and writes in the dirt.

There's no way He can escape acknowledging so great a sin. They know they have Him. They continue pestering Him.

Jesus continues to doodle.

Finally, He glances at the woman, then at the men, and slowly steps aside. Almost as if to say, "Oh, I'm sorry, I didn't mean to interrupt you. You were saying?" Then He speaks, essentially saying, "He who is without sin among you, be My guest. Throw the first stone."

Mic drop.

It's quiet several minutes. The men file out. The temple empties. Jesus is left alone, in the temple, with a naked woman.

Of course, there are no sinful thoughts running through Jesus' mind. He was tempted as we were, yet sinless.[1] Rather, Jesus is comfortable in His house in whatever condition people come to Him.

By now, the cool air has dried the sweat on her skin. Giving rise to goose bumps. Jesus asks, "Woman, where are those accusers of yours? Has no one condemned you?"[2] She shakes her head but won't look up. She's still too ashamed to make eye contact. Jesus lifts her chin. He wants her to see His face. To know the absence of shame. His acceptance. His great love. He shakes His head. "Neither do I condemn you; go and sin no more."[3]

WHERE THE FATHER'S
LOVE FOUND HIM

He stunk. Clothes tattered. Hair matted. Beard stained. One shoe missing a sole. The other worn through. Personal hygiene out the window. Chin, once high, now drags his chest. His eyes scan the ground, afraid to make eye contact lest he bump into a creditor. One front tooth is missing. Another is cracked. The chest full of gold chains is gone. Sold. Gambled. Or stolen. The ring his father once gave him was pawned weeks ago. He is now skinny, ribs showing. Hungry. And he's not just mildly entertaining the idea of what might be in the fridge. He is nauseated and can think of little else. The once lofty air has left the building.

This silent ending had a boisterous beginning. Not uncommon. It sounded like this: "I want what I want, when

I want it, because I want it, and I want it right now." His friends poured gasoline on the fire, and pretty soon he was spitting flames. Angry, spiteful, full of himself, he went to his father. Stared down his nose. Disdain spread across his lips. He spouted: "I want my share. Now." Given the culture, his demand was unconscionable. Sort of like saying, "You are dead to me. I want nothing more to do with you and your silly, pathetic life. I'll take what's mine. From this moment, you're no longer my father and don't ever speak to me again."

Pockets full, he turns his back and, surrounded by a fair-weather posse, walks away. Laughing. Skipping. Slapping backs. Sucking courage from a brown bag. Glorious sin on the horizon.

Behind him, the father stands on the porch, a piercing pain in his chest.

The distance increases. Time passes. A poor fund manager and unwise in pretty much every way, his prodigal living is short-lived. High life leads to low life. The boy lives it up. Drinks whatever. Smokes whatever. Buys whatever. Sleeps with whomever. Whenever. Wherever. He is a man with no control over his spirit. "Like a city broken down, without walls."[1]

To make matters worse, famine enters the story. The writing on the wall becomes clear. Once the sugar daddy has been picked clean, the posse stampedes.

Broke, hungry, alone, and ashamed—but not quite

humbled—he "joined himself" to another.[2] Said another way, he sells himself as a slave. A Jewish boy going to work for a Gentile farmer raising pigs. This is apostasy. He could not be any more unclean. There are laws about this, and he is breaking all of them.

In that pen, surrounded by manure and swarming flies, holding the slop bucket, he stands just one final rung from the bottom.

He stares into the bucket with a raised eyebrow, his mouth watering, thinking to himself, *That's not so bad. I could probably get that down.* Carob pods—sort of a bean-looking thing with the consistency of shoe leather. One of the only fruit-producing plants to actually produce fruit in that area during times of famine. It's a last resort—even for the pigs.

Can you see him scratching his head? Deliberating? Staring around to see who might be watching? This is where he steps off the ladder. Feet on the bottom—of the bottom. He has attempted to pull fire into his bosom, and it is here the third-degree burns are revealed.[3] Not only has he sinned and fallen short, gone his own way, astray, he has missed the target entirely. His righteousness is "like filthy rags."[4] Everything about the prodigal is offensive, and he is paying the price of his offense.

But notice what finds him. There in that muck and mire and sour stench and poor choices and sin piled high, something swims past the reasonable filter of his mind and into the still-tender, yet-to-be-calloused places of his heart. And it's not condemnation and finger-pointing shame. It's the memory of his dad. The love of the father.

Of all places for love to find him.

Desperate for something to eat, our prodigal eats the pods. And then "he came to himself."[5] What better than the bitter, nasty aftertaste of the pod to shake some sense into him. Something akin to a two-by-four to the mule's head.

And then he turns around.[6] He turns his back on his sin and sets his face toward his father. A hesitant jog at first. Then a chin-raising trot. Lungs taking in air.

When he reaches the hill a mile out from the farm, he is sprinting. Arms flinging sweat, a trail of dust in his wake. If you listen closely, you can hear the beginning of a sound emitting from his belly. Low. Guttural. It is the sound of pain leaving his body.

And here's the best part. It's the father. Still standing on the porch. Yet to leave his post. One hand shading his eyes. Scanning the horizon. Searching for any sign of movement.

Something atop the hill catches his eye. He squints. Leans. *Can't be. Too skinny.* A shake of the head. *No swagger*, he thinks to himself. *But . . .* Then a deeper glance as the figure gets closer. Doesn't take long for that signature body language to register. The father exits the porch as if shot out of a cannon. Having closed the distance, the son falls at his father's feet. He is groveling. Face to toes. Snot mixing with tears. "Father, I have sinned."[7]

The father will have none of this. He lifts him, falls on his neck, and kisses him.

The son protests, arm's length. He has yet to make eye contact. "But, Dad, I'm not worthy . . ."

The father waves him off, orders his servants, "Clothe my son! Bring me a ring! Carve the steaks! Raise the tent!"

Servants scatter. The son stands in disbelief. Tattered and shattered.

"But, Dad . . ." The son has come undone. "You don't know what all I've done. I'm unclean. Please forgive—"

The father gently places his index finger under his son's chin and lifts it. Eye to eye. He thumbs away a tear. His eyes speak the words the son has needed to hear since he turned his back. The father pushes matted hair out of his eyes. "You, my son, are my son. Once dead, now alive. All is forgiven."[8]

THE SIGNATURE OF
THE MESSIAH

The crowds are massive. Some twenty miles down from Jerusalem, Jesus is walking into one of the oldest cities in the world, Jericho. Over a period of some five thousand years, something like twenty-six cities have been built here—one on top of another. Jericho sits in the cradle, or intersection, of ancient trade routes, so it's long been a hub of commerce, news, and information.

He's been here many times.

Jericho is buzzing with rumors of a carpenter who can perform miracles. The blind see. The lame walk. The dead are brought back to life. The epicenter for all that buzz is the city gate. News travels from here to the far corners of the globe.

Sitting in the sand is a blind beggar. Given his infirmity, it's the best he can do. He seldom bathes. Smells unpleasant. His hair is matted. Food particles caught in a greasy beard. Clothes tattered. Fingernails need clipping. Feet filthy. He's one of *them*.

His chosen location is strategic. This is storied ground. "The city of palm trees."[1] This is the very gate where Joshua, or Yeshua, the successor to Moses, whose name means "Yahweh is salvation," marched around the city and defeated an enemy with a shout. A spoken word. It is here that Joshua rescued the harlot Rahab, a defiled woman, and all her family because she hid the spies and believed the Lord is "God in heaven above and on earth beneath."[2]

Bartimaeus is blind, not deaf, so he sits by this same gate as another Yeshua comes near. He's no doubt heard about the lepers, now clean. About the lame, now dancing. About the demons, cast out. The five thousand, fed. The paralyzed man lowered through the roof who walked out the front door. The lame man at the pool of Bethesda who picked up his mat. About the woman who bled. No more. And he's heard about Lazarus and how he'd been in that stone tomb four days when the carpenter from Nazareth called him out. He's heard the power of Jesus' words and how He speaks even with the filthy and the defiled. And how He forgives sins.

To say Bartimaeus has been waiting for this day is a bit of an understatement.

As Jesus approaches, the noise of the crowd reaches Bartimaeus's ears. He knows they are still some way off, but he can contain himself no longer. He stands and begins jumping up and down, waving his arms. "Son of David, have mercy on me!"[3] The root of this verbal proclamation is the same truth that delivered Rahab. A belief in the One True God. He shouts again. And again. And again. So much so that the crowd tells him, "Shut up! Can't you see He's busy?"

But that's the point. He can't see.

The term *Son of David* is a messianic claim. By saying it out loud, the speaker is stating for all who would listen that he believes the prophecies about the Messiah coming from the line of David. Ezekiel wrote, "David My servant shall be king over them, and they shall all have one shepherd."[4] (At this point, King David had been dead for 385 years.) Isaiah said, "There shall come forth a Rod from the stem of Jesse, and a Branch shall grow out of his roots. The Spirit of the LORD shall rest upon Him."[5]

He might also have heard of the angel's promise to Mary, the carpenter's mother. "You will conceive in your womb and bring forth a Son, and shall call His name JESUS. He will be great, and will be called the Son of the Highest; and the Lord God will give Him the throne of His father David. And He will reign over the house of Jacob forever, and of His kingdom there will be no end."[6]

He came to know it, this bold messianic proclamation

could get Bartimaeus killed because the Romans have their kings and don't like competition.

They will prove this in about a week.

The disciples are with Jesus. They are headed up to Jerusalem for Passover. Off to the side bounces Bartimaeus, screaming at the top of his lungs. Some in the crowd warn him that he should keep quiet. They want the blind man to shut up, to stop bothering the teacher. As if Jesus has more important things to do.

What is Bartimaeus thinking? Perhaps he is thinking the same thing Isaiah thought when he said, "And in that day shall the deaf hear the words of the book, and the eyes of the blind shall see out of obscurity, and out of darkness. . . . Then the eyes of the blind shall be opened, and the ears of the deaf shall be unstopped."[7] And the same thing Joel thought when he said, "Whosoever shall call on the name of the LORD shall be delivered."[8] And the same thing the psalmist thought when he said, "The LORD opens the eyes of the blind."[9] And the same thing John the Baptist thought when he proclaimed, "Behold! The Lamb of God who takes away the sin of the world!"[10]

Has Bartimaeus heard the story of the paralytic lying on a bed who was brought to Jesus? Has he heard that when Jesus met him, Jesus said, "Son, be of good cheer; your sins are forgiven you"?[11] Does he know that Jesus makes it a habit to eat with tax collectors and sinners? Does he know that when questioned about this, Jesus responded, "Those who are well have no need of a physician, but those who are sick. But go and learn what this means: 'I desire mercy and not sacrifice.' For I did not come to call the righteous, but sinners, to repentance"?[12] Does he know the story of the woman with the issue of blood? Or how He raised the young girl from the dead? Has he heard the story of the blind man at Bethsaida and how Jesus spit on his eyes and healed him?

Bartimaeus will not be quiet. Instead, he jumps higher. Screams louder. Waves his arms faster. Undeterred. Unashamed. Bartimaeus shed his precious dignity for one chance at freedom. One chance to see clearly.

Jesus has waited for this day. He chose this gate. He's been waiting for this moment. And as He rounds the corner, He grins and thinks, *My brother Bartimaeus, I'm coming for you.* The sound of Bartimaeus's voice reaches Jesus' ears, and He stops walking. He commands that the shouting man be brought to Him. The crowd quickly changes its disposition. "Come on. Hurry. He's calling you."

Bartimaeus throws aside his garment. There is no pretense. Nothing to cover his filth. He elbows his way—blindly—through the crowd. People are ushering him forward. "Hurry, He's calling you. He's very busy." Bartimaeus bounces forward like a ping-pong ball. Feet shuffling. Steps uncertain.

Bartimaeus makes it to Jesus' feet, but the only way he can know if he's reached a man that meets the description of

Jesus is to "look" with his hands. To "read" Him with his fingers. He reaches out like Helen Keller at the Alabama pump house and feels Jesus' arms and face, eyes and nose, and then stands back, jaw open, realizing he's just touched the Bright Morning Star. Living water.

Emmanuel. Yeshua. Yahweh Is Salvation. Joshua is once again standing outside Jericho, tearing down walls. Bartimaeus crumbles like a sack of potatoes.

Jesus, surrounded by a growing crowd, looks down, sort of leaning over, the smile growing on His face. He inches closer. Beneath the hovering crowd. "What do you want Me to do for you?"[13] Jesus knows Bartimaeus is blind, but Jesus is not asking for His own benefit. And He's not really asking for Bartimaeus's benefit. He's asking for the benefit of all those people milling around. The folks with their fingers pressed to their lips or their hands in their pockets. The doubters and the haters and the debaters. Jesus wants to encourage them. Challenge them. Wake them up. Why? Because His time is growing short, and this slumbering crowd is waiting for Him to show up while the blind idiot dancing along the wall is declaring before the world that He has arrived.

Big, big difference.

Bartimaeus—forehead on Jesus' feet and lips inches from the dirt—says, "Rabboni, I want to see." That word,

Rabboni, is a term of endearment. By saying it, Bartimaeus is telling Jesus, "My heart is with Yours."

A bright smile appears on Jesus' face. He knows what's about to happen. He loves this stuff. He's living for this right here.

Blind, smelly, begging, cloakless Bartimaeus—whose eyes are fogged over, clouded white, thick with cataracts—is piled up before the promised Messiah. Hands trembling. Jesus puts His hands on Bartimaeus's shoulders. He holds his hands in His own. Jesus fashioned Bartimaeus together before the foundation of the world. He made his very eyes. His lenses. His optic nerves. The carpenter standing in the street made those very eyes from the dust of the earth before the foundations of the earth were laid.[14]

Jesus has been looking forward to this moment. To set it aright. He's missed Bartimaeus.

Jesus kneels, places His fingertips on Bartimaeus's chin, and lifts his face. Then, speaking softly, He says, "Receive your sight; your faith has made you well."[15] The same words He spoke to the woman with the issue of blood.[16]

For the second time in his life, the breath of God falls on the clay that is Bartimaeus. Those words enter his ears, swim around his mind for a millisecond, and then the curtain is lifted. Technicolor, 3D, and 4K pour in. His mind is flooded with light and shape and color and depth and people

and smiles and sky and clouds and perception and . . . *Bam!*
IMAX! 20/20! The face of Jesus.

This all happens near the city gates of Jericho, the "cursed
city."[17]

Jesus is sending a message.

To the world.

Standing in a "cursed city," He speaks to an unclean man
living under a curse. It's a good description of me. Of you.

Some months prior, Jesus had sent a message to John
the Baptist: "The blind see and the lame walk."[18] Among
other things, giving sight to the blind is the signature of the
Messiah. And where does He sign His name? In the dirt at
the Jericho gate on the road to Jerusalem.

Jesus is headed to the cross. He knows this. He is putting not only the physical world but the spiritual world on
notice. When He spoke to Bartimaeus, He drove a stake in
the ground—"I'm coming. And I'm bringing the kingdom
of God with Me."

BY THIS . . .

The sun is down. Darkness blankets Jerusalem. They are reclining at supper. Celebrating the Feast of the Passover. Normally a joyous time. Prior to dinner, Jesus stands and takes off His outer garments. Doing the very thing He did when He left heaven.

> Christ Jesus, who, being in the form of God, did not consider it robbery to be equal with God, but made Himself of no reputation, taking the form of a bondservant, and coming in the likeness of men. And being found in appearance as a man, He humbled Himself and became obedient to the point of death, even the death of the cross.[1]

Jesus ties on the apron of a bondservant—representing a servant by choice and not coercion—and kneels before His friends. The sons of Zebedee hear an echo of Jesus' words in their minds: "Whoever desires to become great among you, let him be your servant. And whoever desires to be first among you, let him be your slave—just as the Son of Man did not come to be served, but to serve, and to give His life a ransom for many."[2] The only sound in the room is that of water spilling over dirty feet, then returning to a basin. One by one, Jesus washes their feet.

This includes Judas.

Jesus scoots over to Peter's feet, and Peter recoils. "You're not washing me, Lord." Jesus continues to disciple His disciple: "For I have given you an example, that you should do as I have done to you. . . . A servant is not greater than his master."[3] These words will be important in a few minutes.

This right here, this Last Supper, this moment when their feet are drying—this is the beginning of the end. He dries their feet, and they recline at the table, but Jesus' heart is heavy, and they pick up on it. Jesus scans His friends. "I do not speak concerning all of you. I know whom I have chosen; but that the Scripture may be fulfilled, 'He who eats bread with Me has lifted up his heel against Me.'"[4] Jesus becomes troubled in His spirit. His face shows it, and He speaks the source of His pain: "One of you will betray Me."[5] The disciples whisper among themselves. They are confused. Peter motions to John, who is leaning against

Jesus' shoulder. Peter asks quietly, "You're closest—who's He talking about?"

John shrugs. He turns to Jesus. "Lord, who is it?"[6]

Jesus replies, "It is he to whom I shall give a piece of bread when I have dipped it."[7] He then dips the morsel and gives it to Judas Iscariot. The Bread of Life willingly giving His body to the one who would betray Him. Forgiveness before the sin. Then, gently and firmly, Jesus gives Judas permission. "What you do, do quickly."[8] At the time, only Judas understood. The rest would in a few hours.

Now, alone with the remaining faithful Eleven, in the last few hours they have together, Jesus captures their attention and says, "A new commandment I give to you."[9]

The word *new* rattles around in their minds.

Jesus—the Lawgiver, the Word, the Alpha and Omega—is speaking with His friends. Each of the eleven men in that room is listening with rapt attention because something new is about to be spoken. Something that hasn't been spoken since Moses disappeared into the cloud and came back shining brilliantly, carrying two stones. The disciples know that these words supersede everything spoken before. As difficult as it is for them to believe it, this new law is more important than and weightier than Moses'.

They lean in. Waiting. Pin drop. The mystery of the universe, the secret of the ages, is to be revealed here. Jesus whispers, "Love one another . . ." He pauses, knowing they will remember this moment for years to come. Then He says quietly, "As I have loved you. . . . By this all will know that you are My disciples, if you have love for one another."[10]

Several of them scratch their heads and ask, "'By this' what?" They think back through the last three years, reminding themselves of the nature of Jesus: He preached, healed the sick, cast out demons, raised the dead, performed miracles. They saw His power—the power of God—but they had yet to understand His love.

But Jesus knows what's coming. He knows what His friends are about to see. He knows the disciples are going to be gutted. Their hearts shredded. They are simply not going to be able to wrap their heads around what will happen. So after dinner, wanting to make sure they heard Him the first time, He says it again: "These things I have spoken to you, that My joy may remain in you, and that your joy may be full. This is My commandment, that you love one another as I have loved you. Greater love has no one than this, than to lay down one's life for his friends."[11]

Fast-forward twenty-four hours.

Jesus' blood drips down His lifeless body and stains the grooves of the cross. The disciples understand exactly what Jesus meant when He said, "By this . . ."

THE COVENANT

Jesus is reclining at the table. John rests on one side. Peter on the other. The rest of the Twelve lie in a circle around Him. It is Passover. Although this one will be a little different. Jesus speaks:

"I have earnestly desired to eat this Passover with you before I suffer. For I tell you I will not eat it until it is fulfilled in the kingdom of God." And he took a cup, and when he had given thanks he said, "Take this, and divide it among yourselves. For I tell you that from now on I will not drink of the fruit of the vine until the kingdom of God comes." And he took bread, and when he had given thanks, he broke it and gave it to them, saying, "This is my body, which is given for you. Do this in remembrance of me." And likewise the cup after they had eaten, saying, "This cup that is poured out for you is the new covenant in my blood. But behold, the hand of him who betrays me is with me on the table. For the Son of Man goes as it has been determined."[1]

Jesus' words puzzle His friends. There's a lot here. Suffering? New covenant? Betrayer? Their heads are spinning. No one wants to be the betrayer. They're worried. Peter asks John to ask Jesus who it is. Jesus dips the bread in the oil and gives it to Judas. "What you are going to do, do quickly."[2] satan[1]* enters Judas, and Judas walks out. No explanation. No goodbyes. It's the last time the Twelve will ever eat together. Notice what Jesus says: He establishes the new covenant with Judas still seated at the table. It's a beautiful picture of the unmerited love of God—Jesus is extending forgiveness before the sin. He is cutting the covenant with the one who will cut Him.

Judas closes the door, and Jesus sits alone with the remaining Eleven. They're confused and have no idea what's about to happen. If they did, they might have acted differently. Interestingly, the next sentence in John's gospel records an amazing observation: "Having received the piece

---

1. This isn't a typo. I refuse to capitalize the names satan and lucifer, and I refuse to capitalize the word he when it refers to satan—even at the start of a sentence.

of bread, he [Judas] then went out immediately. And it was night."[3]

"Night" is an apt description.

BETRAYED

Night has fallen. Darker than usual. Turning cool. Jesus has just finished the Passover dinner. Given His betrayer permission. Watched Judas walk out. Washed His disciples' feet. Taken the cup. The end has come.

The unsuspecting Eleven follow Him through the quiet city streets. Flying high on the heels of the triumphal entry, they are giddy with what might be. The conquering Son of David soon to sit on His rightful throne. Somewhere a candle flickers. Then another. They descend the hill of the city of David, and Jesus approaches the Brook Kidron. Higher on the hill above them, the clear spring bubbles up out of the earth, circulates through the grounds of the temple, and fills the ceremonial cleansing pools. From there it washes out the blood of the morning and evening sacrifices before it descends the hill.

When it rolls beneath their feet, it smells of death. Jesus stands on the stone bridge that crosses the brook. Glancing over His shoulder. The smell fills His nostrils. Fitting.

He enters the garden. Gethsemane. This is the place where the olives are crushed. Where the oil is poured out. This, too, is fitting.

A thousand years before Jesus, Absalom, King David's son—his own flesh and blood—betrayed him. Turned on him. David was forced to flee the city. The people wept and wailed as with one loud voice, and they crossed over the Brook Kidron. "So David went up by the Ascent of the Mount of Olives, and wept as he went up; and he had his head covered and went barefoot. And all the people who were with him covered their heads and went up, weeping."[1]

Jesus has David on His mind. He's thinking about one of the psalms he wrote. Psalm 22 to be precise. Why? Because He is about to live it. Line by line.

Jesus enters the garden with the Eleven. Stomachs full of food and eyelids heavy with wine. "Sit here while I go and pray over there."[2] He took with Him Peter and the two sons of Zebedee. "My soul is exceedingly sorrowful, even to death. Stay here and watch with Me."[3] Despite His pleas, they sleep. Snoring. Smiling smugly. Remembering how all the city laid down their cloaks and sang, "Hosanna to the Son of David! 'Blessed is He who comes in the name of the LORD!'"[4] A song so loud that, had they been silent, even the stones would have cried out.[5] The Eleven are dreaming of their conquering King. A political solution. But their dreams will not come true.

Jesus separates Himself. Prays. He knows the end from the beginning. He is in agony. Listen to King David again: "O My God, I cry in the daytime, but You do not hear; and in the night season, and am not silent."[6]

Jesus returns to His friends only to find them crashed out. Oblivious. Drool running out the corners of their mouths. He shakes their shoulders. They momentarily rally. "Oh . . . so sorry, Lord. You were saying?" He returns to His prayers. Behind Him, they return to their snoring. Face to the ground, Jesus' blood vessels burst and He sweats blood. His heart knows what is coming before His ears can hear. "Be not far from Me, for trouble is near; for there is none to help."[7]

In the distance, the air is filled with the sound and flickering firelight of soldiers. "Rise, let us be going. See, My betrayer is at hand."[8] The stone bridge carries the echoes of swords and shields and whispers. Judas, thirty pieces of silver richer, emerges, smirking. He slithers forward, grabs the Master, and then presses his lips to the face of Jesus.

The seal of betrayal. Of the King of the universe. Of the "heir of all things, through whom also He made the worlds . . . being the brightness of His glory and the express image of His person, and upholding all things by the word of His power."[9]

That very same Jesus—the Ancient of Days—who fashioned
Judas out of the dust of the earth and then pressed His lips to
Judas's face and breathed in the breath of life, the *ruach*, has
just allowed the created to betray the Creator.

What kind of a king does this?

The prophets had said this was coming. None better than
Isaiah:

> Who has believed our report?
> And to whom has the arm of the LORD been
> revealed?
> For He shall grow up before Him as a tender
> plant,
> And as a root out of dry ground.
> He has no form or comeliness;
> And when we see Him,
> There is no beauty that we should desire Him.
> He is despised and rejected by men,
> A Man of sorrows and acquainted with grief.
> And we hid, as it were, our faces from Him;
> He was despised, and we did not esteem Him.
> Surely He has borne our griefs
> And carried our sorrows;
> Yet we esteemed Him stricken,
> Smitten by God, and afflicted.
> But He was wounded for our transgressions,

He was bruised for our iniquities;
The chastisement for our peace was upon Him,
And by His stripes we are healed.
All we like sheep have gone astray;
We have turned, every one, to his own way;
And the LORD has laid on Him the iniquity of
    us all.
He was oppressed and He was afflicted,
Yet He opened not His mouth;
He was led as a lamb to the slaughter,
And as a sheep before its shearers is silent,
So He opened not His mouth.
He was taken from prison and from judgment,
And who will declare His generation?
For He was cut off from the land of the living;
For the transgressions of My people He was
    stricken.
And they made His grave with the wicked—
But with the rich at His death,
Because He had done no violence,
Nor was any deceit in His mouth.
Yet it pleased the LORD to bruise Him;
He has put Him to grief.
When You make His soul an offering for sin,
He shall see His seed, He shall prolong
    His days,

And the pleasure of the LORD shall prosper in
   His hand. . . .
Therefore I will divide Him a portion with the
   great,
And He shall divide the spoil with the strong,
Because He poured out His soul unto death,
And He was numbered with the transgressors,
And He bore the sin of many,
And made intercession for the transgressors.[10]

KING OF THE JEWS

He is stumbling now. A trail of blood marks His serpentine path on the narrow street out of the city. The wood is heavy, but that's not what's crushing Him. Three-inch thorns are pressing into His skull. Much of the flesh has been removed from His back, neck, and sides. The local rulers want to make an example of Him. A public deterrent. A public execution on a well-traveled road just outside of town. They also want to shame Him, and they have. He's completely naked.

By 9:00 a.m. He's outside the gate. On the outskirts. Out where they burn the trash. Somebody from the crowd spits on Him. Another plucks out a handful of His beard and reminds Him of all the ridiculous things He said leading up to this moment. A third suggests that if He really is who He says He is, then He should be able to do something about it. All talk. No action.

A group of fishermen watch from a distance. Pained faces. Breaking hearts. The road rises, and the bleeding carpenter stumbles to His knees. He tries to stand, falls again, and one of the soldiers comments how this could take all day. The soldier eyes a North African man in the crowd, points a sharp sword at the heavy wood, and commands, "Carry that."

Simon steps onto the road, kneels, and black hands lift a bloody cross. Face-to-face with the condemned, he's never seen anyone so marred. So grotesque. The two whisper words no one can hear as they slowly trudge forward.

Behind them the town is readying for a feast. The place is packed. A few hundred yards away in the temple, the high priest is preparing the sacrifice. Sharpening his knife on a stone. The morning incense wafts heavenward. Fresh showbread has replaced yesterday's display. Simon carries the wood until the soldier tells him to drop it. When he does, soldiers slam the condemned Man onto the wood and stretch wide His arms. Two men hold His hand in place, one swings a hammer. The nail pierces His wrist, separating the bones. His screams echo off the enormous rocks that make up the city walls.

Out of respect for His nakedness, the women have gathered at a distance. His mother is inconsolable. A second woman stands nearby. Nobody really knows her name. All we know is that for the last twelve years she has bled constantly. Making her an outcast. Defiled. Unable to enter the temple. She spent her life savings on a cure with no relief. Then she met the condemned. Clung to the "wings" of His shirt. Now she doesn't bleed anymore.

The soldiers drive skinny spikes through the Man's other hand and both feet; they lift the wood. Like Moses lifting the serpent in the wilderness.[1] Gravity tears the flesh as they unceremoniously drop the cross into a hole. A sign above Him, written in Greek, Latin, and Hebrew, reads "King of the Jews." He is flanked by two common and dying men.

The crowd is larger than usual for a morning execution. A fact not unnoticed by the soldiers. A beggar named Bartimaeus watches through tears. Having heard of the trial and the invented charges, he walked the road up from Jericho. Some twenty miles through the night. A short time ago, the two met at the city gate. Bartimaeus had been begging because he was blind. Then he met the Man. Told Him, "I want to see." Ever since, Bartimaeus has had perfect vision—but now he doesn't like what he sees.

Nicodemus is here, as is a man named Lazarus, who stands quietly with his sisters. His story is of some renown because he died and had been decaying four days when the criminal called him out of the cave. Even he has a tough time believing his own story. A young man, a former paralytic whose friends had lowered him through the roof of a crowded house where the criminal was staying, paces nervously nearby. A centurion stands quietly off to one side. Respectful. He's not with this garrison. A man under authority, he's come to pay his respects. Standing in the shadows, an angry fisherman waits impatiently. One hand on the hilt of his sword. As the hours pass, the other fishermen grow more vocal. Barabbas is here too. He is a murderer. Released just this morning from a death sentence. He stands in the shadows, in utter disbelief.

Fights break out in the crowd. The soldiers grow nervous. Reinforcements are summoned and sent.

Last week, the criminal claimed that zeal for His Father's house consumed Him. Now He's consumed by torment. Painted in His own blood. It trails down His body and drips into the dirt where the earth silently swallows the crimson stain. Above, up on the crosses, the three condemned men have a conversation. Something about paradise. One believes. One does not. Clustered on the road nearby, the soldiers play a game. Wagering for the Man's clothes. Over the next few hours, the Man suspended on the middle cross pushes up with His legs, pulls with His arms, and tries to fill His lungs with air. Each breath harder than the last because His lungs are filling. He grows weaker.

It's not long now.

Many in the crowd are weeping. They've torn their clothes. Mourning the leader of a failed rebellion. Earlier in the week, the entire town was ready to install the Man as ruler. Shouting. Waving palm branches. Throwing down their clothes. Praising the One to take on Rome. Even the rocks cried out. But the Man made outrageous claims. Didn't back them up. A flash in the pan. Now He's a nobody. Shamed. Rejected. Bruised. Crushed. Little more than a common, nameless criminal. A grain of wheat falling to the earth.[2] The song of drunkards.[3]

For the last three hours, an eerie darkness has spread across the earth.

His mother approaches, hanging on to the arm of one of the fishermen. The dying Man speaks to both. She buries her face in the other man's shoulder. Her knees buckle, and he holds her. She is shredded. They retreat, and the Man is thirsty. A soldier dips a sponge in something sour and holds it to the Man's mouth, but He refuses. A scribe, a learned man, watches the hanging Man refuse the sponge and thinks to himself, *Could it be . . . ?* as the words of a psalm echo in his mind: "For my thirst they gave me vinegar to drink."[4]

With considerable effort, the Man lifts His chin off His chest and scans the crowd. His breathing grows shallower. He is drowning. Summoning His last ounce of energy, the Man pushes up one last time and screams heavenward. A shadow falls across Him, shrouding Him in darkness. Even God has forsaken Him.

In the temple, the high priest slices the throat of the lamb and catches the warm blood in a basin.

On the road outside the gate, the condemned Man exhales, dies, and gives up His spirit.

Below, the earth quakes. Above, the sky falls pitch dark. A light in the heavens has been turned off.

No. *The* light.

The crowd huddles in hushed silence. Lightning flashes and spiderwebs across the sky. The air turns cold. Nearby, a soldier shakes his head, whispering something about the Son of God.

The two men on either side are dragging it out. To speed things along, soldiers swing heavy bars and break their legs. No longer able to push up, the condemned drown quickly.

With little more to see, the soldiers disperse the crowd. The criminal hangs alone. Dead. Eyes still open. The life that had been there moments ago is gone.

Blood still drips off the toes of His left foot. The words of Moses echo: "For the life of the flesh is in the blood, and I have given it to you upon the altar to make atonement for your souls."[5]

The lifeless Man hangs at an odd angle, and His bones seem out of joint. Off to one side, His mother won't leave. She is screaming at the top of her lungs. Abruptly, a soldier shoves a spear into the chest cavity of the dead Man, and water and blood spill out from the hole. The splashing sound echoes. The earth trembles and shakes with angry violence. The stones of the temple are rocked. The curtain tears in two. The sky thunders and lightning flashes. The sign above His head reads "King of the Jews."

THE FATHER'S SILENCE

It's the ninth hour. Jesus hangs from the nails. He's struggling to breathe. Drowning in His own lung fluid. Too tired to pull or push Himself back up. The holes in His hands and feet are stretched. His shoulders and probably several of His ribs are "out of joint."[1] Dislocated. He has been punched in the face; His beard has been plucked out; He's been beaten by rods; and three-inch acacia thorns have been shoved into His skull. The skin, muscle, and sinews of Jesus' back, sides, and face have been ripped off by a Roman scourge. Blood drips off His toes. When Isaiah said His "visage was marred more than any man,"[2] or He was unrecognizable as a man, this is that moment. He's also naked. Completely.

Here hangs the righteous, sinless, spotless, obedient Son of the Most High God. The One who knew no sin, who became sin for us.[3] Who "has borne our griefs and carried our sorrows."[4] Despised, smitten, stricken, afflicted, pierced, crushed, scourged, oppressed, cut off from the land of the living, assigned a grave with wicked men, crushed by His very own Father, sent here for this very purpose. Intentionally put to grief. Knowing anguish. Pouring out His soul to death. Bearing the ages on His shoulders.

Below Him, the soldiers are not impressed.

The Roman army is the most powerful in the world. Also the largest. The logistics of supporting and maintaining an army that expansive required planning and forethought. An occupying force had to be fed. And a fed army had to go to the bathroom. Which led to sanitation concerns. Disease and bacteria would spread like wildfire if not contained. In order to help stem the flow of sickness and maintain a sanitary army, soldiers were issued two things: a jar of vinegar and a *tersorium*. Or, sponge on a stick. After using the bathroom, they would dip the sponge in the vinegar, clean their backside, and repeat as needed. You can see where this is going.

"Immediately one of them ran and took a sponge, filled it with sour wine and put it on a reed, and offered it to Him to drink."[5]

Some have suggested the sponge in the mouth was an act of mercy, having been dipped in opium-laced vinegar. We don't know that. And given the soldiers' treatment of Jesus until now, I highly doubt it. What we do know is that

Roman society used sponges on sticks as toilet paper, and there on the cross they shoved it in Jesus' mouth. "Eat this and die!" It tells us what they thought of Him. This continued mockery would be consistent with the soldiers' attitude toward Jesus throughout His crucifixion—save one.

Until now, He hasn't opened His mouth. Silent as a lamb led to slaughter. But somewhere in here, Jesus cries out. Screams at the top of His lungs. Just a couple of words, but if you listen carefully, the words betray the emotion. The wound. Jesus the man is talking. "My God! My God!" Another lift. A shallow inhale. A frantic look. Until now, perfect, He and the Father had known unhindered communion. The two had been one. But now they are not. He screams. "Why have You forsaken Me?"[6]

Jesus has never done a single thing wrong. Ever. He is totally obedient. In all things. And for some reason, this same Jesus has just been rejected by the Father. For the first time in His life, He is alone.

In the ninth hour, all the weight of the world's sin, the billions of us on this planet, all our black-hearted stuff, has been dumped on the carpenter's shoulders. And God looks away.

Jesus knows rejection. Deeper and more painful than any of us have ever known or experienced. "Jesus cried out with a loud voice, saying, 'Eli, Eli, lama sabachthani?' that is, 'My God, My God, why have You forsaken Me?'"[7]

Forsaken. One word tells us all we need to know.

When Jesus needs His Father most, the Majesty on High is nowhere to be found.

Jesus' one phrase is a verbatim quote of the beginning of Psalm 22. He is reciting the first line, expecting all who are listening to fill in the rest.[8]

Everyone standing around Him knew what He was saying: "Dad, I'm crying out but You don't answer. I'm a worm. Not even a man. I'm a reproach. Despised. People are sneering at Me. Bulls have surrounded Me. Their mouths are open like a ravenous and roaring lion. I don't have much left. I'm poured out like water. All My sockets are dislocated. My heart is melting. My strength is gone. My mouth is dry. My tongue sticks to the roof of My mouth. Dogs circle Me. They've pierced Me. They're gambling for My clothes. I won't last another five minutes!"

This is the Son of Man crying out to the Father.

Until this moment, Jesus and God the Father had known unhindered union. Perfect intimacy. The sinless Son had done everything asked of Him. As these words leave His mouth, the Lamb of God is currently carrying away the sins of the world. He is our propitiation. Pouring out His soul. Here, in this very moment, Jesus has become sin.[9] If ever there was a moment in human history when a father was proud of a son, it is this one. And yet, in this moment, the Father is silent. Offering no response.

Here, for the first time, Jesus knows something He's never known. And it is this "knowing" that kills Jesus. Yes, the crucifixion would have eventually done the job,[10] but Jesus, Savior of the world, dies with a broken heart. A shattered soul. And the autopsy will show that the King dies of the deepest, most painful wound of the human soul.

Rejection.

The fluid in His lungs has reached the tipping point. Jesus has but one breath remaining. What will He do with it? He arches His back, tightens His lips, and speaks a singular word: "And Jesus cried out again with a loud voice, and yielded up His spirit."[11]

What did He say? What did He cry out? Seems like His last word would be important. Maybe we should listen. John tells us: "So when Jesus had received the sour wine, He said, '*Tetelestai!*' And bowing His head, He gave up His spirit."[12]

Tetelestai.

The final word spoken on earth by the King of all kings.

PROPITIATION

On a cross on the earth below, the Son of Man dies. Innocent blood shed. Payment made. In full. Mankind redeemed. Forever.

The Father—watching His Son die a gruesome and painful death—opens His mouth and releases the pain and agony He has known while His Son was away. He entrusted His Son to us and yet we on the earth despised Him, shamed Him, and considered Him smitten and stricken by God. Nothing could be further from the truth.

Lightning flashes from His throne, sending bolts to the earth below; the heavens thunder, and the light that once shone on the earth falls dark. Stones split and an earthquake shakes Jerusalem. Having waited patiently since the garden of Eden, God the Father reaches down into the holy of holies and rips the veil in two with His very own hands.

That veil is His Son.[1] God once again dwells with man.

Heaven erupts. The angels of God come unglued. The Son has returned. Victorious. He alone has done what no one else could. "Once for all time, the just for the unjust, so that He might bring us to God, having been put to death in the flesh, but made alive in the spirit."[2]

After a thirty-three-year absence, the Son has returned. He's in bad shape. Every sin that has ever been committed by anyone at any time, or ever will be after this moment, is draped around His shoulders. Shoved like a spear into His chest. Soaked through and through. Infused with His DNA. "He made Him who knew no sin to be sin for us."[3] Sinless God is now identified totally and completely with sin. Nothing could be more horrific.

And yet Jesus walks in. This is Mount Zion, the city of the living God. Heavenly Jerusalem.

The Holy City sits on a high mountain. It is radiant. Clear as crystal. It has a great high wall with twelve gates. Angels guard each gate. And on the gates are written the names of the twelve tribes. The walls have twelve foundations, and on the foundations are written the names of the twelve apostles. Its walls are jasper, pure gold, clear glass, covered with every jewel, and the city's streets are gold. Nothing unclean is here. In this city there is nothing detestable, false, unfaithful, or untrue. There is also no sun or external light source. God the Father is the source. This means no shadows. No unlit space.

The door is open. A throne sits at the far end. Miles away. Covered in jasper. Carnelian. An emerald rainbow surrounds the throne. Twenty-four elders, clothed in white, lie flat on their faces. They, too, have thrones, but when Jesus walks in, they launch themselves off their seats and bury their noses in the ground at His feet. The golden crowns they once wore have been cast at His feet. As He approaches, lightning flashes, thunder sounds, and seven torches of fire stand before the throne, surrounded by a sea of glass and crystal. Four creatures sit on each side. The creatures possess eyes fore and aft. One is a lion, one an ox, one a man, and one an eagle in flight. Each has six wings. Twenty-four hours a day, seven days a week, they say, "Holy, holy, holy, is the Lord God Almighty, who was and is and is to come!" The elders lie prostrate in agreement. "Worthy are you, our Lord and God, to receive glory and honor and power." They proffer space, time, and matter. "You created all things, and by your will they existed."[4]

Innumerable angels are arrayed in festal gathering. They are here for Him. His return. This is the assembly of the firstborn, which He is. They worship continually before God, the judge of all. High and lifted up, righteousness and judgment are the foundations of His throne. He is a consuming fire. Always has been.

Walking in, carrying His own blood in a cup, Jesus has proven that He alone is the faithful witness. The firstborn of the dead. He is the second Adam, born on the cross when the soldier shoved the spear in His chest, and blood and water flowed.

In this moment, He is the ruler of every king everywhere. In this moment, He is undefeated, and His victory is undisputed and irrevocable. The angels are about to lose their minds. The Father has inched forward to the edge of His throne. His right foot is tapping. His pulse has quickened. He's had about all He can take. The next person to lay a finger on Jesus will be incinerated—ten thousand degrees Fahrenheit in less than a millisecond.

Through a rescue mission, a prisoner exchange, Him for us, Jesus has freed, ransomed, and redeemed people of every tribe, tongue, color, and nation—from their sins with His very own blood. Having made the journey there and back, the King has returned. And He has brought mankind, all of captivity, with Him. In the distance, He sees the construction that has taken place in His absence. His Father's house. Rooms have been added. Lots of rooms. He smiles. He loves family. Can't wait to share it.

There are two sounds: Jesus' footsteps and the pounding of His Father's heart. Every muscle is tense. Coiled. This place is about to explode in an expression of joy unlike any ever.

Jesus is not just a King. He is *the* King. And He's not just the ruler of a kingdom. He is the ruler of *the* kingdom.

To Him belongs all power and authority and dominion, and in the next few seconds He will do something no king anywhere has ever done. He will transform and transfer the nation of slaves He ransomed into a kingdom of priests— priests to His God and Father. And then in His first act as King, He will do the unthinkable. The unimaginable. He will give His friends the authority He is given. Making them sons. Coheirs. With all the rights and privileges thereof.

These are the last steps of a journey that started back in the garden of Eden. Before, even. Jesus has come to make a payment. Final payment. In blood. His own. This propitiation ushers in those who believe in His name to serve alongside Him as priests before His God and Father.

Every eye is fixed on Him. He alone has done this. This is Jesus. The Alpha and the Omega, the First and the Last, who is and was and is to come. When He last left, He was clothed with a long robe, a golden sash around His chest, hair white like wool, like snow, His eyes a flame of fire, His feet burnished bronze, His voice like many waters. He holds seven stars in His hand, and from His mouth comes a sword. His face is like the sun shining in its strength.

But here and now, He is the Son of Man. Returning to His Father. He is "marred more than any man, and His form more than the sons of men."[5] With every step, His visage becomes more disfigured. By the time He reaches the throne, He is unrecognizable as a man.

It's not far now. Just a few more steps. Before He left, He humbled Himself and did not think equality with God something to be grasped. And He does not now, which is why He alone has been lifted up and given the name above every name. Before Him, there is a river flowing from the throne of God. Those who want to get to the Father must wade the river. No exceptions. Except Jesus. He walks on top. On either side is the Tree of Life, with twelve kinds of fruit, producing fruit each month, and the leaves are for the heal-ing of the nations.[6] As He walks, He speaks: "I am coming soon, bringing my recompense with me, to repay each one for what he has done. . . . Blessed are those who wash their robes, so that they may have the right to the tree of life and that they may enter the city."[7] He glances outside the city. Outside of heaven. To the darkness covering His execution below. "Outside are the dogs and sorcerers and the sexually immoral and murderers and idolaters, and everyone who loves and practices falsehood."[8]

Jesus is not just closing the distance to His Father. He is mediating a new covenant. A "better covenant . . . established on better promises."[9] The blood of the old cov-enant cries up from the ground, "Guilty!" Which is true. We are. Every last one of us. But in His hand He carries the blood of the new covenant, which He has cut with mankind. One that fulfills every requirement, thereby establishing it as new. In it, He is both the Just and the Justifier. The blood of this new covenant whispers, "Innocent." Jesus' voice thunders and shakes the earth.

In His hands, Jesus holds a cup. It is the cup His Father gave Him. The cup of wrath. Now filled with His very own blood. As He approaches the throne, He holds out the cup for all to see. One final act. He turns it up and paints the mercy seat. Seven times. The blood drips from the pores of His sweat, to His beard that was plucked out, to His face that was struck by fist and rod, to His brow stuck with thorns, to His back where the flesh was torn off in chunks, to His hands and feet pierced with nails, and finally to His side split open by a spear. Jesus puts Himself on display for the entire universe to see, the complete shedding of His blood.

Propitiation.

—✦—

God the Father launches Himself off His throne. At the speed of light, He wraps His Son in His arms and covers His face in kisses. Not because He is the prodigal returned but because He is the righteous Son who by His very own blood has healed God's hurting heart. The heart of the Father that was broken in the garden when Adam and Eve fell. God the Father has wanted for so long to walk once again with the man and woman He created; and now His Son, His only

Son, has bought back mankind, ransomed and redeemed, and erased the barrier wall erected by the sin of mankind. The Son has justified man and brought mankind back into the presence of a holy God and Father.

God the Father is healing Jesus' wounds. One by one. Tending tenderly to His Son. When the Father gets to Jesus' hands and feet, and the hole in His side, He fully intends to close up the holes. Make all things new. But then Jesus looks up at His Father, laughing. He says, "Abba, given their unbelief, maybe You should leave those open. Because if You close them, they'll never believe it's Me."

With His divinity now uncloaked, Jesus is visible as fully God and fully man. His eyes are flames, and diadems rest on His head. He has a name that God gave Him but only He knows. He wears a robe dipped in blood, the train of which fills the temple, and the name by which He is known to us is "the Word of God." The armies of heaven are seated on white horses and arrayed in fine linen, white and pure. Their attention is trained on Him, and they await His singular order. A sword extends from His mouth with which He will strike down nations. From His throne and with His scepter, He will rule with a rod of iron. He treads the winepress of fury of the wrath of God Almighty. On His robe and on His thigh is written a name, the King of kings and Lord of lords.[10]

God Most High places a handkerchief in His Son's chest

pocket. With it, He will wipe away every tear. The end of mourning has come. No crying. No pain. Jesus looks down at us and smiles. "I am making all things new."[11]

Having made payment, Jesus turns and stares across the sulfur lake that burns with eternal fire and speaks to the souls held in prison. "I am the Alpha and the Omega, the Beginning and the End."[12] He holds out His hands, and in them are springs of water; it's free. No one has to pay. Those who conquer, who endure, will drink from His hand. He will be their God and they will be His people. But to those who say no, the cowardly, faithless, detestable, murderers, sexually immoral, sorcerers, idolaters, and all liars, they will join satan in the sulfur lake. Eternal fire.

A book is opened before Jesus. On the cover is written "The Lamb's Book of Life."[13] It's the only copy. With His mouth He writes the words.

While darkness covers the earth below and His body is moved into a freshly cut grave owned by a rich man, Jesus' work is not yet done. He has somewhere else to go.[14]

Before Jesus leaves, God the Father—the Ancient of Days, clothing white as snow, hair pure wool, throne wreathed in fiery flames—speaks. And as He does, fire comes from His mouth. A thousand thousands serve Him. Ten thousand times ten thousand stand before Him. The Son of Man is presented before Him, and God Most High presents the Son before every tongue, tribe, nation, and person. Then

He grants Him all authority and dominion and glory and a kingdom. The Father speaks so everyone can hear, "From now on, all peoples, nations, and languages will serve You. Your dominion is everlasting, and it will never end, and your kingdom can never be destroyed."[15]

A wrinkle forms between Jesus' eyes. He is staring into hell. He holds up a finger and says, "This won't take long. Be right back."

ENTER THE KING OF GLORY

Jesus descends and walks through the gates of hell, where demons and spiritual forces of wickedness throw blood-stained metal and bronze and run out of the crowd to punch Him or stab Him with swords, to whip Him or thrust spears completely through Him. The road is littered with bones and maggots and rotting flesh. The pandemonium rises as He approaches the throne where satan has placed himself. The raucous party is at a climax. The noise deafening. The stench nauseating. The evil horde has created a mosh pit, and they are foaming at the mouth because they think they are about to feast on the body and blood of Jesus the Christ.

The only one not enjoying the party is satan. he knows the prophecies; he knows the Word; he was there when God spoke it. satan is not happy. In truth, he is squirming; he's been dreading this day. Trying to find a way out. A way around. A legal loophole. his eyes are frantic. he is looking for a way out because he knows he is about to be exposed as the fraud he is—and always has been.

Jesus walks down the road to satan's court. Hordes of demonic entities hang on the rafters and balconies around Him. They are taking turns on the ceiling fans that do little to alleviate the heat. Everything that is evil is in attendance and salivating at the coming final blow, which they know will eradicate Jesus once and for all. Total, universal, otherworldly domination! In their minds, they have salted and peppered the body and are turning Him over the spit. They can taste Him.

But a funny thing happens here.

It is here—in the pit of hell—that Jesus strips off the sin of humanity that has masked Him. Like a dark blanket, or cloak, He rips it off His shoulders and hurls it like Halley's comet at the skeletal throne comprising skulls and vertebrae on which satan has parked his fat self. The light shoots forth from Jesus' body, and the darkness rolls back like a scroll. Demons screech and writhe. Those closest to Jesus go up in smoke. Literally. Ten thousand degrees Fahrenheit in less than a second. Just dark spots on the dirt where their souls once stood.

Party's over. satan turns and kicks it into high gear, cowering. he's defeated. Powerless.[1] Dethroned. Destroyed.[2]

Disarmed. Made a public spectacle.[3] Exposed as a punk whose kingdom is crumbling all around. Jesus, the Word made flesh, who upholds all things by the word of His power, says, "Stop!" and lucifer can't move. he knows what Jesus came to get. Jesus lifts the keys dangling on lucifer's belt. "I'll take those." Then He places His heel on satan's neck and speaks for all eternity to hear. All of this universe and every other can see and hear His proclamation. His thundering voice sounds like many rushing waters. Right here and right now, Jesus is ruling in the midst of His enemies, who have been made His footstool.[4]

The Lion of Judah roars, "All debts are paid. All past, present, and future claims are canceled. Forever. 'The life of the flesh is in the blood, and I have given it to you upon the altar to make atonement for your souls.'[5] I have bought mankind back with My blood. My children are justified, redeemed, sanctified. No longer slaves. I have snatched them back out of the hand of the deceiver. Sin no longer has dominion. My children are no longer under law but under grace!"[6]

Face down, satan lies in excruciating pain. he writhes as Jesus' foot presses his mouth into the maggot-filled, worm-crawling dirt of hell. satan raises a finger. "But what about that scum-sucking sinner, Charles Martin?"

Jesus nods and considers me, then He squeezes His hand like a sponge. Given the hole, it should have produced blood.

At least a drop. But there was none. Not one single drop. "Nope."

satan protests. "But what about that thing he did . . ."

Another squeeze. Nothing. Evidence that, on the cross, Jesus held nothing back. He'd left it all topside. Bled out. "Paid in full."

satan reaches in his pocket and holds up the record of my wrongs of which I was and am guilty. Every last one. The claims were true then.

They are true now. I'm guilty as sin. Jesus reads it. "You got them all. No, wait, you missed a few. But . . ." Again, He holds His hand. One last squeeze of the sponge. The hole is dry. Veins empty. "Your claims are revoked."

Jesus, dangling the keys, makes one final declaration, carving it into the walls of hell with His very voice. "Be it known this day—all is forgiven. I have redeemed mankind with My blood on the altar. It is finished."

Upon hearing the words of Jesus, the foundations of hell crack and crumble. satan's throne crumbles. The kingdom is in chaos.

Gone is the tortured carpenter. Gone is the heavy, lumbering, splinter-laden cross, the nails still dripping. It's been snapped like a toothpick. Reduced to splinters. It doesn't hold Him anymore. Neither does the grave. This right here, this is Jesus, the firstborn among the dead, the victorious, conquering, undefeated King—who holds the keys to death and hades.

satan's defeat is absolute. The victory complete. Eternal. Irrevocable.

As Jesus walks out of hell, He exits through the prison of cells—the Alcatraz of hell—where His people have been held in bondage. Slavery. Every form of addiction. Every sin. And as He walks by, every lock clicks, shackles fall off, gates of bronze are ripped off their hinges, bars of iron cut in two.[7]

Prisoners, long held captive, begin screaming at the top of their lungs. "Freedom!" and "Long live King Jesus." "Worthy is the Lamb that was slain!" "Worthy to receive honor and glory and praise." "The King of glory has come!"

Jesus is laughing. Tears streaming down His face. He knows the prisoners by name. He has missed them. Every last one. He watches their twisted and bent bodies exit, straighten, stretch, and put one foot in front of the other. Walk. Jog. Run. Kicking up dust. A mass exodus. Dying of thirst, they drink from His hand. Clear living water. Those who don't drink, drown.

Having freed all who want freedom, Jesus stares topside. At His tomb. At those weeping. He can see their broken hearts. His own heart yearns. He can't wait.

Now the fun begins.

The Son of God brushes the dust off His feet—and returns.

THE BORROWED TOMB

An earthquake shakes Mount Zion. The ancient stones cry out. The veil in the temple is torn in two. The crowd falls pin-drop silent. Many cry. Groups huddle together. All shake their heads. "Surely, He was the Son of God."

Their eyes focus on Him. Lifted high. Silhouetted against the sky. Just "as Moses lifted up the serpent in the wilderness, even so must the Son of Man be lifted up."[1] He hangs unrecognizable. Bloodless. Crushed. Lifeless.

Sabbath is approaching. If they don't get Him off the cross soon, He'll have to hang, by law, until Sabbath is over. Their hearts are shredded. Mary Magdalene is weeping uncontrollably, clawing at the dirt.

A rich man, Joseph of Arimathea, who had become a disciple, uses his status to gain access to Pilate. "I am here to ask for the body of Jesus."

Happy to be rid of him, Pilate waves him off. "Take Him."

In muted whispers, and careful not to rock the body, the men slide the cross out of its hole and set it down. They peel off the crown, pull out the nails, and some brave soul reaches up and closes His eyes. One by one, they stare at Him. The absence of His voice is unbearable. *How can this be?*

The soldiers are impatient, and the time for goodbyes is over. With an armed escort, they carry Jesus' body to a new tomb, which Joseph had hewn out of the rock. Inside, they lay the very dead and now decaying body of Jesus down on a cold shelf. His skin is pale, grayish in hue; His lips are purple, and His face ashen. Dark, caked blood trails down His legs and toes. The hour is late. Long shadows stretch along the ground. No time to wash the body. Through tears, they kiss His forehead and wrap Him in clean linen grave clothes. After saying their goodbyes and praying over the body, they walk out only to watch as a large stone is rolled against the door of the tomb, leaving Jesus' flesh and bones to lie in darkness.

Walking away from the tomb, the images flashed back across their minds. The depth of their sorrow was more than their hearts could grasp. *How could this have happened? How did He let it? He healed the sick. Raised Lazarus. Why?* Their last image of Jesus was of a Man dying in anguish and torment, screaming out at the top of His lungs.

Seemingly helpless. Powerless. His body ripped and torn. Inhuman suffering.

In their minds, the unfathomable had happened. Jesus had lost. In the minds of those who loved and followed Him, Jesus had lost everything.

Walking away from the cross, from Jesus' tomb, as they wiped away tears and swore at the memory of the soldiers, as they plotted and planned, each asked one impossible question: "What now!?"

For these simple two words, they had no answer. No game plan. All they could do was shake their heads and fists. No one, not even Peter, James, or John, had an answer. They did not know what we know. All they knew was that the Lamb of God who takes away the sin of the world, the hope of all mankind, the One who came to sit on the throne of David, the One who healed the sick, walked on water, drove out demons, the One who raised the dead to life— could not defeat death. Could not save Himself. He was gone. And they were left to mop up the mess.

CAN IT BE?

S hrouded in shadow, Peter is spinning his sword on its point by its handle. His sweat has dried. His tears have not. He hasn't eaten. Hasn't slept. The wine does little to medicate the pain. He sits alone on a hill. Before him lies the tomb that holds the body. Soldiers hover like hornets. They've driven an iron spike into the wall of the tomb behind the stone. Sealing it. Preventing the stone from being rolled back. They're passing the wine around, retelling the story. Laughing. Slapping backs. One in particular cleans the tip of his spear. An odd mixture of blood and water. Another sits quietly by himself, shaking his head. He keeps staring heavenward. Muttering something about the Son of God. But he is the minority. A third sits atop the round stone, dangling his feet.

The Man inside the tomb lies wrapped in cloth. A hasty job. His lips are blue, hair matted, body cold.

Graveyard dead.

Peter is mumbling. Talking to himself. He glances over his shoulder at the empty cross. Awaiting the next victim. He curses. "Should have been Barabbas. That murderer." Peter cannot wrap his head around the last seventy-two hours. He is tormented by questions: *What happened? Why did He let it?* and *What now?* But maybe the most painful question of all has to do with himself. *How could I?* As daylight approaches, a nearby rooster crows. Again. He covers his ears. *Somebody should kill that thing.* But what good would it do? He knows that every single day for the rest of his life he will never escape the sound or the memory.

Peter spins the sword again. The thought of it takes him back to the garden. The night of the unlawful arrest. When he cut off the ear of the high priest's servant. His friend's words made no sense then. They make less sense now. "Put your sword into the sheath. Shall I not drink the cup which My Father has given Me?"[1] Peter shakes his head. *What cup?* He continues mumbling. "But what about the kingdom? What about us? What about me?"

Peter has never known shame like this. It's more than he can bear.

A few blocks away, the mother of the dead Man stares down at her hands. The same hands that held Him when

He nursed as an infant. That tucked Him in on cold nights when He was a boy. That dried His tears when He skinned His knees. That taught Him how to make bread. That held His face when she kissed Him. The same hands that pointed to the pots of water at the wedding in Cana only three and a half years ago. "Do what He says." Her sorrow is unmatched in human history.

She is close to losing her mind.

Across town, another Mary, Mary of Magdala, is crying. Brokenhearted. A bubbling mixture of pain and anger. Of unvented rage. They falsely accused Him. Unjustly arrested Him. Played out a mock trial. Stripped Him. Shamed Him. Beat Him mercilessly. Tortured Him. Shoved the sponge in His mouth. Then they just stood there, laughing, gambling, while He screamed at the top of His lungs. *Why didn't He do something about it?* Nothing He said came true. His words seemed so full of life when He spoke them. Now they're just as dead as He is. He could heal the sick, raise the dead, cast out demons, but when the time came, He could not save Himself. *What kind of God would do that to a man? Much less His own Son?*

Mary keeps looking over her shoulder as she turns a singular question over in her mind. The further she gets from Jesus' last breath, the more the fear torments her. And in this moment, it is raging.

Scattered about town, the defeated band of rebels are

hurting. Living in hiding and fear of Rome, they have no answers. Rent down the middle. Trying to pick up the pieces. The disillusionment is suffocating.

The chief priests and elders are feeling smug. Secure. They slap each other's backs. Nod knowingly. Feeling justified that they have honored God, for no one can call himself the Son of God. The law forbids it. There's a ruckus at the door. Without warning, a former follower, a mealymouthed weasel of a man named Judas who turned rat and betrayed the deceased, returns. Guilt-riddled. He holds out the blood money. "I have sinned by betraying innocent blood."[2]

They couldn't care less. He's a pawn. They're incredulous. "What is that to us? You see to it!" Judas throws down thirty pieces of silver.[3] The payment for his services. Distraught, he runs to a known field, climbs a tree, ties a noose, and jumps. Death by suffocation. By hanging. His body swings alone. But the tree limb he chooses is weak, so as his decomposing body swells in the hot sun, it breaks the limb, sending the man's body to the earth where, upon impact, it splits open, spilling his intestines on the ground. Hearing of this, and not wanting to add blood money to the temple treasury, the religious rulers later buy the field and call it *Akeldama*, or Field of Blood.[4]

The psalmist spoke of this very field a thousand years prior, and to this day, it is desolate and no one lives in it.[5]

Jerusalem is quiet. Save the drunk soldiers in Pilate's

garrison who are singing, still rolling their eyes at the pathetic so-called *King of the Jews*. They pass the wineskin. "What a joke!"

In the temple, the priests eye the veil. Inexplicably torn in two by the earthquake.

Throughout the night, Peter sits on the edge of a vineyard and stares down at the tomb. Owned by a rich man. He is lost in a slideshow of memories. Of words spoken. He is trying to remember the sound of his friend's voice, but the sound is fading. All he can hear is the echo of His cries. Screaming in pain at the top of His lungs, Peter tries to quiet the voices of regret and shame, but he cannot. In his mind's eye, the blood continues to drip. Just outside the round door of the tomb is the knee-deep depression in the rock where the vineyard workers crush the grapes to make the wine. Peter closes his eyes and buries his face in his hands. Arrested in an olive garden. Buried in a vineyard.

Oil and wine.

⚊✦⚊

Daylight is less than an hour away. Mary of Magdala can sit still no longer. She has to do something. What she wants is a few minutes alone. To talk to the body. Tell Him goodbye. Joined by Mary the mother of James and Joseph (who is also the sister to Mary the mother of Jesus), Salome,[6] and Joanna

117

the wife of Chuza, Herod's steward,[7] she walks through the darkness, carrying embalming spices. Intent on properly preparing Him for burial. Knowing that the stone is some five feet tall, and that the tomb is sealed with an iron spike, they ask the obvious, "Who will roll away the stone?"

But there's a problem.

In the darkness, they can just make it out. The seal is broken. The iron spike has been snapped in two. Like a toothpick. The massive stone rolled away. Soldiers gone. An eerie quiet blankets the garden. Mist rises off the earth. Mary Magdalene steps inside. Trembling. Her worst fears realized. She cannot breathe in or out.

The body is gone.

Mary rubs her eyes. Her heart breaking further. Her anger grows and she aims it at the soldiers who left their post. A singular question spins in her mind. Jesus delivered her from seven demons. She heard Him tell them to go. And when He did, she felt them wrench her, heard them scream in a voice that was not hers though it used her mouth, and she knew when they physically departed her body. She felt them leave. Since then, she has known and walked in freedom. But then she saw Him die.

And if He's dead, are the demons coming back?

He could deliver her, but not Himself. So what about the seven? Are they coming back? And if so, are they bringing more with them like Jesus said they would?[8] Is that what she has to look forward to? Was her deliverance only temporary? What torment awaits her?

Needing to see, she pokes her head inside the tomb. To her surprise, two angels sit at either end of where the body had lain. She doesn't know whether to fall down or start swinging. She eyes the angels. Suspiciously. One of them speaks: "Why do you seek the living among the dead? He is not here, but is risen!"[9]

The mental picture of dead Jesus returns to Mary's mind. *Unrecognizable as a man.* Mary sucks in a breath. She rolls up a sleeve and braces herself. This could get ugly. But the word *living* bounces around inside her head. If true, no . . . it's too good to be true. She can't let herself go there. But if it is . . . no, she can't let herself think that. It could just be a sick trick. Everyone knows Herod is crazy. She wouldn't put it past him.

The glowing man in white continues. "Remember how He spoke to you when He was still in Galilee, saying, 'The Son of Man must be delivered into the hands of sinful men, and be crucified, and the third day rise again.'"[10]

Somewhere in that fog, Mary remembered His words.[11]

The words He is risen ramble about her brain. She mouths the words. Trying to connect the meaning. Then she voices them out loud. Little more than a whisper. "He is risen."

About then it hits her.

Mary hikes up her dress and bolts back to town. Knees and elbows pumping like pistons. Caught between belief and unbelief, hope and despair, and unadulterated rage, she flings open the door and tells the disciples everything she has seen and heard.

Peter and John race outside the city. John, evidently the faster runner, arrives first. He stoops down, sees the folded linen but, afraid to enter, stops short. Peter arrives next. Breathing heavily. Hand on the hilt of his sword, he barges in. Peter's eyes fall to the face cloth that had been around the dead Man's head. Now it lies neatly folded in a place by itself. Why would the soldiers take the time to do that? But the women spoke of talking angels, and neither Peter nor John see anything other than an empty tomb. They conclude that the women are distraught. Delirious from their pain.

They return to their homes.

Save one. Mary.

And she is close to losing her mind.

She stands for a moment weeping outside the tomb. When she stoops to walk in, the angels have returned. She tries to flag down Peter and John, but it's too late. They ask her, "Woman, why are you weeping?" The unspoken impression being, *"We already told you He's not here."*

Unable to make sense of any of this, she cries, "They have taken away my Lord, and I do not know where they have laid Him."[12] *My Lord.* Even now, Mary's proclamation is that Jesus is Lord. An amazing declaration given that nothing in her circumstances agrees with her.

Mary turns and bumps into the gardener. Finally, someone normal she can speak to. His voice is calm. Soothing. Like water. "Woman, why are you weeping? Whom are you seeking?"

Controlling her grief, she says, "Sir," and points at the tomb. Her finger is shaking. Tears and snot are pouring off her face. "If You have carried Him away, tell me where You have laid Him, and I will take Him away."[13]

Then, in what is certainly the single greatest moment in Mary's life, the man cracks a smile. He speaks, and Jesus uncloaks His divinity. "Mary!"[14] And in that single word, the voice and person of Jesus has returned.

He is alive!

Mary reaches out and touches His face. Her fingers read His smile.

Mary screams, "Rabboni!" and launches herself airborne, catching Jesus across the chest. Wrapping arms and legs around Him. Smothering His neck in kisses.

Jesus catches her and laughs. Certainly the most beautiful laugh in the history of laughter. He, too, is excited to see her. He's missed her. He knows she's been hurting. They all have. He can't wait to see them. And He would have gotten here sooner but had to take care of a few things first. He sets her down. "Do not cling to me, for I have not yet ascended to the Father; but go to my brothers and say to them, 'I am ascending to my Father and your Father, to my God and your God.'"[15]

Jesus was dead. Mary had seen it. With her own eyes. Mary had watched Him pray the prayer of a dying man: "Into Your hand I commit my spirit."[16] Then she watched Him push up on His nail-pierced hands and do just that. She witnessed the soldier's spear pierce His chest and heard the sound of blood and water flowing and splattering. She had helped take Him down off the cross. She had worked hastily to prepare Him, but they didn't have time. While the soldiers had yelled at her from the doorway and told her to hurry up, she had spilled tears on His cold, dead, rigor-mortis-stiff, blue-lipped, blood-caked, ashen body.

Mary saw Jesus doornail dead.

But now He's not. Jesus is alive. Speaking. And Mary knows it. She just heard His voice. Saw the light in His eyes. Felt the warmth of His skin.

He spoke to her. She felt His breath on her face.

This changes everything. About everything.

ON THE ROAD TO EMMAUS

Jesus draws near and begins walking with them. And just as He did with Mary in the garden, He has cloaked His divinity. They cannot recognize Him. Jesus asks, "What kind of conversation is this that you have with one another as you walk and are sad?"[1]

Cleopas is dumbfounded. He scratches his head and looks at Jesus as if He's not in touch with reality. "Are You the only stranger in Jerusalem, and have You not known the things which happened there in these days?"[2] Everyone knew. The death of Jesus was no quiet execution on a hidden street corner. Just as Moses lifted up the serpent in the wilderness, so Jesus was lifted up. All Israel saw it. Rome too.

Jesus, not ready to reveal Himself but wanting to keep the conversation moving as they walk, says, "What things?"

"And they said to him, 'Concerning Jesus of Nazareth,

a man who was a prophet mighty in deed and word before God and all the people, and how our chief priests and rulers delivered him up to be condemned to death, and crucified him. But we had hoped that he was the one to redeem Israel. Yes, and besides all this, it is now the third day since these things happened. Moreover, some women of our company amazed us. They were at the tomb early in the morning, and when they did not find his body, they came back saying that they had even seen a vision of angels, who said that he was alive. Some of those who were with us went to the tomb and found it just as the women had said, but him they did not see.'"

Jesus responds, "O foolish ones, and slow of heart to believe all that the prophets have spoken! Was it not necessary that the Christ"—Christ and prophet are not the same, and the Christ is about to show these two why and how—"should suffer these things and enter into his glory?' And beginning with Moses and all the Prophets, he interpreted to them in all the Scriptures the things concerning himself."[3]

After He interpreted the Scriptures for them, "they drew near to the village to which they were going. He acted as if he were going farther, but they urged him strongly . . ."[4]

His words had rekindled their hope. And their faith.

They pleaded with Him, "'Stay with us, for it is toward evening and the day is now far spent.' So he went in to stay with them. When he was at table with them, he took the bread and blessed and broke it and gave it to them. And their eyes were opened, and they recognized him."⁵

The Bread of Life. Handing out life. It was the last thing He did before He walked to the cross and the first thing He does upon His return.

Having once more uncloaked His divinity and revealed Himself, He "vanished from their sight. They said to each other, 'Did not our hearts burn within us while he talked to us on the road, while he opened to us the Scriptures?' And they rose that same hour and returned to Jerusalem. And they found the eleven and those who were with them gathered together, saying, 'The Lord has risen indeed, and has appeared to Simon!' Then they told what had happened on the road, and how he was known to them in the breaking of the bread."⁶

Good news wouldn't wait, so they walked back seven miles through the night to tell their friends.

THE DO-OVER

Jesus tells the disciples to return to Galilee. So they do. Peter, Thomas, Nathaniel, James, and John, and two unnamed disciples. Unlike the rest, Peter has a problem. A self-inflicted wound. A telephone pole sticking out of his chest. And Jesus is about to expose and heal it.

Peter, opening his big mouth once again, announces to the group, "I'm going fishing." They all pile in the boat with him. He's returning to his former life. Fishing for fish. His shame has convinced him that he's disqualified himself for the life to which Jesus had called him. One and done and all that.

Jesus is having none of this. Just as Jesus crucified every assault the enemy could level at us, He is about to show Peter (and those around him . . . and us) that He wasn't kidding when He said, "It is finished!"[1] And that "finishing" includes shame, regret, and self-inflicted wounds.

They fish all night with no luck. Jesus, again having cloaked His divinity so they can't recognize Him, stands on the beach and yells, "Children, have you any food?"

They corporately answer, "No."

He laughs. "Cast the net on the right side of the boat."[2] The implication is "Do what you're not doing."

Not knowing who He is, they look at Him with squinted eyes. These guys fish for a living. They're pros. They know what they're doing. They mumble among themselves. "Who's this guy think He is? Left or right side doesn't matter." Nevertheless, they cast the net, and, wonder of wonders, they are unable to haul it in it's so full of fish. A foretelling of what's to come. Of what's about to happen.

Sensing that something is amiss, John scratches his head and says to Peter, "It is the Lord!"[3]

You think?

Having stripped down for work, Peter is standing in his undergarments. Hair pulled back in a ponytail. Sweat dripping off him. Seeing the Lord, he puts on his outer garment—and takes a swan dive off the bow. He doesn't ask the Lord to tell him to come to Him so that he might walk on water. Not this time. He doesn't feel worthy. Shame is crushing his spirit. Peter is a mess. He swims to shore and walks up on the bank. In the meantime, his fishing buddies row to shore, dragging the filled-to-capacity net.

Onshore, they see Jesus cooking fish—over a charcoal fire.

Smoke rises from the beach. The smell of fish cooking. Peter sees the fire and freezes. Ice water trickles through his veins. That night returns. He remembers sitting around the fire in the high priest's courtyard. He denied the Lord in front of that fire. Peter's heart shatters on the beach. From the mountaintop victory at Caesarea Philippi and Peter's vocal proclamation to Jesus and the whole world, "You are the Christ,"[4] he has bottomed out here. Sea level. The single greatest failure and betrayal of his life, and Jesus is bringing him back to that moment. With a charcoal fire. Peter shakes his head.

Jesus speaks over His shoulder, "Bring some of the fish that you have just caught."[5]

Peter grabs the net and singlehandedly hauls it to shore where somebody counts out 153 large fish. Jesus tells everyone, "Come. Let's have some breakfast."

Jesus takes bread and fish and gives it to them. They're elated to see Him. All save one. They sit down alongside Jesus. Like old times. Only they haven't quite grown accustomed to this whole risen-from-the-dead thing. He appears. Walks through walls. Disguises Himself. Disappears. Speaks. Eats. They still don't know what to make of all this. Don't know what'll happen if they get too close. All they know is that He's alive; but they still don't know what to do with the rest of their lives. They are lacking direction—and none more so than the big, mouthy guy in the middle.

Peter is sitting by himself. His hair dangling down over his eyes so Jesus can't see the whites. Peter is afraid to look at Him. Despite his braggadocious claims to the contrary, he did the very thing Jesus said he would do after promising not to. Sitting on the beach, Peter is a liar and a backstabbing coward. Better than no one.

Which makes him a perfect disciple.

Jesus fills a plate and sits down. Shoulder to shoulder. He hands Peter the plate. Peter pushes the fish around. Afraid to look up. His heart is breaking. He wants to vomit. Jesus leans in. His face inches from Peter's. "Peter . . ." Jesus glances at the men spread across the beach. "Do you love Me more than these?"

The implication is clear. Before Jesus' crucifixion, Peter said he did. What happened next? Imagine a man on a rescue mission. Saving prisoners. All of them. Once they are free, our hero hears the helicopter coming. He makes it to the evac zone. Sees the helicopter. Waves at the pilot, who gives him a thumbs-up and tells him "good job." Then, just as the hero thinks he is about to climb aboard and be airlifted to safety, the pilot pulls up on the stick and disappears while the enemy in the grass surrounds our hero and shoves their bayonets through his chest.

This is exactly what Peter did to Jesus. He pulled up on the stick and watched as the enemy pierced His side.

Peter knows exactly what Jesus is referring to. It's all he's been thinking about. Can't get it off his mind. Peter won't look at Him. He nods. "Yes, Lord." He exhales. His chest is tight. A shallow inhale. "You know that I love You."

Peter sets down the plate and finally looks at Jesus. Tears pouring down his face. He is shattered at his own betrayal. His bottom lip is trembling. Snot is pouring out his nose. In his spirit, he is begging his friend, his Lord, his King, to take him back. Give him another shot. End this misery. For the first time, Peter knows how truly unworthy he really is, and yet he is sitting at the feet of his King, asking for a return to the team, to the lineup, when he knows he doesn't have a leg to stand on. "Please take me back. Please, Lord, give me one more chance."

Jesus will do one better. It's why He's here. He loves this stuff. Almost as much as He loves Peter.

Jesus presses His forehead to Peter's. Friend to friend. Brother to brother. Jesus knows the ache of Peter's heart. It's why He built a charcoal fire. To take him back to the moment. But to heal the wound, He's got to pick the scab. Only then can He dig out the shrapnel. Jesus holds Peter's face in both His nail-pierced palms and speaks softly, "Feed My lambs."[6]

Somewhere in here, it strikes Peter that Jesus is restoring him. Bringing him back in. He's no longer an outcast. He's forgiven. Further, he's been charged with tending and feeding sheep. That makes him a shepherd. Something he is now uniquely qualified to be since he understands lost sheep.

Jesus is not finished with him. Not by a long shot.

Peter's desire—the singular cry of Peter's heart—is to show Jesus that he loves Him. Jesus knows this. So He looks into the future and gives Peter a glimpse. He wraps His arm around Peter and says, "Most assuredly, I say to you, when you were younger, you girded yourself and walked where you wished; but when you are old, you will stretch out your hands, and another will gird you and carry you where you do not wish."[7]

Jesus is speaking of Peter's death.

Peter has been broken. Jesus knows this. He is telling Peter He can see the future, and in the future, Peter does not and will not deny Him as he did before the cross. He'll finish the race. Keep the faith. He'll die the same kind of death.

Peter weeps. That he is counted worthy to suffer for Christ and that Christ knows it. He wants nothing more. This is the greatest news he could ever hear.

Finally, Jesus, in perfect grace-filled, forgiving, pulling-for-us, lover-of-our-souls fashion, speaks to Peter the first words He ever spoke to him. And He does it after wrapping His arm around him and bringing him back into the fold. As if He's saying, "Enough of this foolishness. Let's get on with it. We have work to do. There's stuff to be done."

He leans in, and once again the *ruach* of God is breathing life into one of His own. He could have said anything. The same voice that upholds all things by the word of His power and spoke ten trillion stars into the universe and calls each by name is whispering the only two words Peter's heart needs to hear. He makes eye contact, smiles, and whispers, "Follow Me."[8]

For the first time since that night, Peter drinks in a deep breath with no taint of smoke. He holds it. One second. Two. Then he lets it out slowly.

For Peter, this is a do-over. The most beautiful do-over in the history of do-overs. And Peter, to his great credit, takes it and never looks back.

Peter is free. From himself. From his past. From his pain. And from his shame. Two simple words shattered its hold. Peter has been welcomed back in. He is now what he once tasted and has always wanted to be.

Peter is a child of God.

WHAT NEXT?

The sun is setting. A crimson line trails across a blue canvas. The air is cool. A breeze filters through. Jesus and the disciples exit Jerusalem, cross the Brook Kidron, walk through the garden of Gethsemane, and begin the ascent up the Mount of Olives. This is the same path Jesus walked after His arrest en route to His mock trial, His merciless beating, and a criminal's cross. Now they're walking it in reverse.

And all of them recognize it.

The Eleven are laughing and shaking their heads. They're having a difficult time reconciling what they're seeing. Weeks ago, they watched and listened as Jesus died a gruesome death. When they took His body down, some brave soul reached up and closed His eyes. Then they carried His tortured and graveyard-dead body to a cold tomb and watched helplessly as the soldiers rolled the heavy stone into place and sealed it with an iron spike. It was the end of all things good and beautiful.

But that was before.

Now they're walking alongside Him. Huddling close. Touching Him. Making sure. Listening as the laughter enters and exits His lungs. During His earthly ministry, Jesus was a jungle gym for the young. They climbed all over Him. Rolled in the grass. Played tag. Now the disciples watch in wonder as Jesus carries one of their children on His shoulders. Skips along the trail. Sings with another.

They wind up the worn path to a hilltop that overlooks all of Jerusalem. Jesus has been here many times. He has prayed here, wept here, and it is here that His sweat turned to blood. It is here that His blood began crying a better word than that of Abel. And it is here that He told his disciples to wake up. There's a time for sleep, but this was not it.

Over the last few weeks, Jesus has opened their minds to the Scriptures. Allowed them to see what has remained hidden for so long. Blown their minds with each new revelation. To the south sits the city of David. The city of the Great King. Up that winding path, King David returned the ark of the covenant to Jerusalem. The spoken words of God returning to the city of God.

But here and now, that very Word is flesh and walking among them.

Jesus Himself. Eating. Laughing. Talking. Praying. And

not one of them can explain it. It's simply too good to be true. In their minds, anything is now possible. Jesus, the only begotten Son of God, lived, died, was buried, and was resurrected. He walked out of the grave. They don't understand everything that means, but at a minimum it means Jesus is more powerful than death. They are on the cusp of something great. Never seen before.

This is storied ground. Mount Moriah. The mountain of God. The word *Moriah* itself means "foreseen by God." Over there, Abram met Melchizedek in the valley of the five kings; over there, he laid his son Isaac on the altar and raised the knife. This is the mountain of which Abram spoke when he told his son, "God will provide for Himself the lamb for a burnt offering."[1] Down there is the threshing floor of Ornan the Jebusite where God withdrew the plague from the people. Up there, King David brought the ark of God into the city of David. Over there, Solomon built the temple. Along that trail, Jesus rode into the city triumphantly seated on a donkey, and down there, under cover of night, He was arrested. On that serpentine path that winds out of the city, the innocent King carried a criminal's cross. And up there, over by the skull, He poured out His soul unto death. Just over there, His body was laid and sealed behind heavy stone. Three days later, out of that same rock, He rose again—in accordance with everything written before.

More has happened—and has yet to happen—on this

mountain than any mountain in the world. It is here, on this mountain, that the very rocks cry out. It is here, on and in this ground, that God Most High, possessor of heaven and earth, has placed His name. Forever. And it is here that He will, at a future time of His choosing, prepare a lavish banquet for all peoples. Refined and aged wine. Choice pieces of meat. On this mountain, He will swallow up the covering that is over all people. Even the veil that is woven into the nations. On this ground and in His time, He will swallow up death, wipe away every tear, and remove the reproach of His people from all the earth.[2]

But that time is not yet.

And while this is storied ground, these are not storied men. At least not yet. They will be, but here on this mountain they're second string. The did-not-measure-ups. The could-not-cut-its. While they're good Jews, they're not straight As and valedictorians. That's why most are fishermen. This does not mean they weren't smart. Far from it. Most could probably recite entire portions, verbatim, of the Law, the Prophets, and the Psalms. But to be a Pharisee, you had to be something special. A-team. And these men were not. In the world's eyes, these men were your average Joes. B-team.

Which was Jesus' intention all along.

As they climb the hill, their minds spin with possibilities. Most want to stick it to Rome. They are waiting for Jesus to bring down fire from heaven. Elijah-and-the-prophets-of-Baal sort of stuff. Given what they have seen the last few weeks, each has a question on the tip of his tongue. They all want to know the same thing. One of them voices it: "Lord, will You at this time restore the kingdom to Israel?"[3]

Ever patient, Jesus smiles and continues climbing up the mountain. Halfway up, He turns: "It is not for you to know times or seasons which the Father has put in His own authority. But you shall receive power when the Holy Spirit has come upon you; and you shall be witnesses to Me"— Jesus points to the land laid out before them—"in Jerusalem, and in all Judea and Samaria, and to the end of the earth."[4]

Up there, the disciples can see what He's pointing at, but they don't really understand what He's saying. The words rattle around their brains. Words like *Father*, *power*, *Holy Spirit*, and *witnesses*.

They want something more concrete. They want to know when He will send lightning bolts through the chests of Pilate and Herod. They've got it coming. Their days are numbered.

What the disciples cannot see are the myriad angels that have arrayed around them. Resplendent white. Gold. The army of God has come on assignment. To escort the Son home. Banners. Musicians. Dancers. Warriors. They line the mountain. They line the city. They line the earth for miles. Each has six wings. With two they cover their faces. With two they cover their feet. And with two they fly.[5] A living picture of worship and service. At the top of the mountain, God's very own chariot awaits. Driven by white horses.

Jesus can see this. They cannot.

Nearing the top, Jesus walks alongside each of His followers. Holding their hands. An arm around their shoulders. They're all here: Peter, John, James, Andrew, Philip, Thomas, Bartholomew, Matthew, James the son of Alphaeus, Simon the Zealot, and Judas the son of James. His natural brothers are here too. Including James. As is Mary Magdalene and His mother, along with many other families. Jesus is not distant. Not indifferent. Not aloof, standing over there. He's a hugger. He is in their midst. He kisses their necks. Tickles their children. They can feel His breath on their faces.

A breeze blows. It is time. The Father has waited long enough. Jesus turns, looks longingly at His city, at those He loves, and then down through time at you and me. He smiles. He knows the end from the beginning. Then He steps into His chariot, a cloud envelops Him, and He is lifted out of their sight, taking the breeze and the host with Him.

Silence rains down on the mountain.

†⊷⊱✦⊰⊶†

The Mount of Olives fades behind Him. The earth He made grows smaller. A blue dot. Home grows larger before Him. The return trip is quick. The Son of Man enters the gates of heaven wearing a loincloth. Thunderous, raucous praise erupts from a hundred million voices. Streets of gold are lined twenty and thirty rows deep. Everyone hoping to get a glance. *The King of glory has come in.*

He is returning to His Father.

Angels fling wide the doors to the outer courts. Inside, it's standing room only. A sea of heavenly bodies. The sea parts, and Jesus walks through. A straight line. Michael and Gabriel bow and pull on the massive door to the throne room. At the far end, twenty-four elders lay prostrate, noses to the floor, having cast down their crowns at His feet. The chorus is earsplittingly beautiful.[6]

The Father is standing. Eyes singularly focused.

The Son of God enters. He is standing in a river. Or rather, on it. Hovering.

The Father eyes the Son and launches Himself off His throne, closing the distance like lightning. His feet barely touching the ground. When He reaches Him, the Father covers the Son's face in kisses. The Father welcoming home the spotless Son who has done what no one else could. He has ransomed humanity with His very own blood. He alone has prevailed to open the scroll. The Father whispers in His ear, and only the Son knows what He says.

In seconds, they are laughing, dancing, flinging sweat from their brows. Perfect union.

The mansion is larger. Rooms added. Space enough for

every last one. The Father leads the Son to His throne. Everything is just as He left it. Following the Father's invitation, the Son puts on His robe, straps His sword on His thigh, places His ring on His finger, returns His crown to His head, and takes the scepter in His hand. King and priest.

The celebration begins.

—•—⚔—•—

Minutes pass. Nobody says a word. Children run to and fro through the grass. He has come and gone so many times lately, walked through walls of stone, surely this is one of those times.

But standing on that mountaintop, the disciples begin to wonder. And so the longing begins. The longing for His return.

When the smoke clears, two angels stand in the place where Jesus had stood. Dressed in white robes. They are nearing eleven feet tall. Towering. Powerful. Magnificent. One of them speaks: "Men of Galilee, why do you stand gazing up into heaven? This same Jesus, who was taken up from you into heaven, will so come in like manner as you saw Him go into heaven."[7]

The disciples stand speechless, one singular question on the tips of their tongues. No one is yet brave enough to voice it. But each is thinking it: *Just what on earth do we do now?*

To answer this question, they will spend, devote, and sacrifice the rest of their lives. But standing on that storied mountain, in the bosom of the world, they find no answer. As the sun falls over Jerusalem, they return down the mountain, scouring their hearts in search of an answer. And it is about here that they start remembering the words He said while He was with them. They spent three and a half years with Jesus as He traveled and spoke. Jesus often said the same thing in several locations. They had heard the Sermon on the Mount dozens of times. It was something of a stump speech for Jesus. Given this, they could recite His words from memory. Finish His sentences. Which is good. They'll need them in the days to come.

In His absence, they return to Jerusalem—an indescribable combination of sadness and joy. They pray. Sing. Share meals. Encourage one another. And they remember His words: "But you shall receive power."

So they wait.

Given the loss of Judas, they cast lots; Matthias, a long-time follower and believer, is now numbered with the Eleven. The chosen apostles once again number twelve. In total, the disciples number about 120 persons.

Those who stuck with Jesus. Those who saw Him perform miracles, heal the sick, cast out demons, raise the dead, and bounce children on His knee. Those who laughed with Him, cried with Him, and sat on the edge of their seats listening to His every word. These are those who saw Him dead and then saw Him alive. And while they wait, this unlikely and unremarkable group of people begin to reconstruct the words He spoke. Trying to both remember and share that remembrance. As they piece it together, they are amazed at how the Scriptures support and reveal what Jesus said and did. When they stand in the temple and the Scriptures are read, they are astounded. All of the Law, the Prophets, and the Psalms point to Jesus. A jigsaw puzzle of words that begins to take shape.

How could they not have seen it before?

Given a healthy fear of both the Romans and the religious elite, they remain in Jerusalem and keep to themselves. Despite their new revelation into His words, they have a problem. Jesus gave them His authority and commanded them to do as He did, but currently they are powerless to obey Him, and they know it. His words echo: "But you shall receive power when the Holy Spirit has come upon you."[8]

THE HELPER COMES

The wait drags on. A week passes. The disciples begin trying to remember what He said while He was still with them. Then the memories return: After He washed their feet the night before He was crucified. The last words He spoke to them as a group. The last words of a man who knew He was going to die: "And I will ask the Father, and he will give you another *Helper*, to be with you forever, even the *Spirit of truth*, whom the world cannot receive, because it neither sees him nor knows him. You know him, for he dwells with you and will be in you. I will not leave you as orphans; I will come to you. Yet a little while and the world will see me no more, but you will see me."[1]

Upon hearing this, Judas (not Iscariot) spoke for the group. "Lord, how is it that You will manifest Yourself to us, and not to the world?"[2]

It's an honest question, and everyone was thinking it.

Jesus answered him, "If anyone loves me, he will keep my word, and my Father will love him, and we will come to him and make our home with him. Whoever does not love me does not keep my words. And the word that you hear is not mine but the Father's who sent me. These things I have spoken to you while I am still with you. But the *Helper*, the *Holy Spirit*, whom the Father will send in my name, he will teach you all things and bring to your remembrance all that I have said to you."[3]

Then, just to make sure they were listening, Jesus said it again: "But when the *Helper* comes, whom I will send to you from the Father, the *Spirit of truth*, who proceeds from the Father, he will bear witness about me. And you also will bear witness, because you have been with me from the beginning."[4]

Before He was arrested, hoping to make it sink in, He said it a third time: "It is to your advantage that I go away, for if I do not go away, the *Helper* will not come to you. But if I go, I will send him to you. And when he comes, he will convict the world concerning sin and righteousness and judgment: concerning sin, because they do not believe in me; concerning righteousness, because I go to the Father, and you will see me no longer."[5]

Waiting in the upper room, the disciples know they are waiting on Someone, but they don't have much to go on. They do know He will come from the Father, He will teach them, bear witness about Jesus, and help them remember what Jesus told them while He was with them. They also know He will be a Spirit, He will help them and empower them (but in what way they're not sure), and He will convict the world, but that's about all they know.

And given their experience with Jesus, they have no idea what's about to happen.

So they wait.

Who's in the room? Peter, John, James, Andrew, Philip, Thomas, Bartholomew, Matthew, James the son of Alphaeus, Simon the Zealot, Judas the son of James, several women, Mary the mother of Jesus, and His brothers are there. They are filled with joy,[6] and there is unity with the group as they devote themselves to prayer.[7]

For about a week they wait. They keep the door shut due to a healthy fear of Roman soldiers doing to them what the soldiers did to Jesus. Finally, the day of Pentecost arrives.

There are a lot of Jews in Jerusalem. Certainly the most since Passover. The Feast of Weeks is one of three times during the year when all the Jewish males are commanded to appear in Jerusalem.[8] The streets are swimming with observant Jews from out of town.

⊷ ⋈ ⊶

Now let's turn our attention to the kingdom of heaven. Specifically, the throne room. The seat of God Most High, possessor of heaven and earth. The Ancient of Days. After a thirty-three-year absence, Jesus, the only begotten Son of God, has returned. The sinless Son has come home.

All of heaven, hundreds of millions in attendance, wait at the door with bated breath. They are giddy with expectation. God the Father sits on His throne tapping His fingers. The angels drive the chariot homeward, through the first heaven, through the second, and into the third—the throne room of God. The epicenter of this universe and every other.

The chariot stops at the doors to heaven, and Jesus exits wearing what He wore when He left—a loincloth. The King is returning to the Holy Jerusalem. Doorkeepers whisper, "Welcome home, King of all kings . . . King of Glory," and then swing wide the doors where all of heaven hits their faces. Prostrate. Laid out. Every lip pressed to the crystal-clear floor of heaven. Hands raised. Infinite worship. Every voice singing "Holy is the Lord" at the top of their lungs. Jesus returns. He's home.

No sooner has His foot cleared the threshold than God the Father launches Himself off His throne. He will wait no longer. He crosses the expanse of heaven in a thunderbolt, wraps His arms around His Son, and covers His face in kisses. Smearing the tears He has held for thirty-three years across a face that had been marred more than any of the sons of men.

Before all of heaven, God the Father welcomes home the obedient, righteous, spotless, victorious, conquering Son.

Heaven erupts. The roar is deafening. The elation inescapable. Jesus lifts chins, hugs friends, kisses children, laughs, sings. Then like David before the ark, Jesus dances to the throne. Where the elders have yet to come off their faces. Where their crowns have been cast at His feet. Jesus dances through heaven. Flinging sweat from His fingertips. Joy untold. Children join Him, twirling in circles, climb on Him like a jungle gym. Mothers and fathers laugh, sing, cry. The Son is home! He did it. Jesus won. He defeated . . . everything.

He ransomed and redeemed all of mankind with His very own blood. Forever. Rendering an irrefutable and irrevocable defeat to the enemy. Reaching God's throne, the Father clothes His Son. A banquet awaits. He is given a new robe. His train fills the temple. Sword. Ring. Crown. Diadem. Jesus' hair is white. Eyes flames of fire. Feet burnished bronze.

During the clothing, God the Father glances at the wounds in His hands, feet, and side. It's obvious He doesn't like them. They have no place in heaven. The Father touches each tenderly, ending at the hole in His side, then He speaks a word, and the wounds disappear. No scar. No residue. Jesus is perfect. All of heaven rejoices. Angels swing from the rafters. Millions upon millions upon millions dance, sing, laugh. Unhindered freedom and inexpressible joy. Jesus joins in and works His way through the crowd. The rumble of the Father's laughter is heard and felt one heaven down.

One thing remains. The Father grants His kingdom to

His Son and gives Him the seat to His right. And then He gives Him the name at which every knee will bow and every tongue confess. Jesus is not just the ruler of a kingdom. He is the ruler of *the* kingdom. He is all-powerful, all-knowing, and everywhere—both inside of time and outside of it. There is no power that can contend with His. And on His throne, His enemies have been made His footstool. He is the only King, and there is no other.

A week passes, and as the celebration continues, the Father turns to the third member of the Godhead. His Spirit. Holiness is His name. The Father intends to make good on His promise. The Spirit hugs the Father and the Son. They have been together since the beginning. The Spirit hovered over the waters at creation, and nothing that has ever been created was created without the Spirit. He has been intimately involved in every creative act performed at the will of the Father. And on the earth below, His next creation awaits. Possibly His most beautiful. His most magnificent.

The Father turns to the Spirit. "You ready?" The Spirit looks to and fro across the earth beneath. Scanning all of mankind. Throughout the ages.

There is much work yet to be done. He nods. "Been ready." The Father laughs, opens His lungs, fills them to capacity, and exhales. The roar of heaven. A hurricane absent the carnage. The sound shakes the foundations of the mountains and the oceans on earth beneath.

The Spirit smiles. He's been waiting eagerly for this moment. He loves to create, and because of the shed blood of Jesus, a new creation awaits. He is giddy with the thought that He gets to press His lips to those who will receive Him and fill them with His breath. To take up residence within. To dwell inside. To share the love of and intimacy with the Father. He exits the throne room with a swan dive, careening to earth like a lightning bolt, bathed in the shouts, cheers, and cries of victory. At the speed of both light and sound, He roars His way earthward. To His new home. The new temple that is man.

And there in Jerusalem, oblivious as to what, or rather who, is coming, the roof starts to shake. And it sounds like a freight train is about to split the room down the middle. "They were all together in one place. And suddenly there came from heaven a sound like a mighty rushing wind, and it filled the entire house where they were sitting. And divided tongues as of fire appeared to them and rested on each one of them. And they were all filled with the Holy Spirit and began to speak in other tongues as the Spirit gave them utterance."[9]

There were dwelling in Jerusalem Jews, devout men from every nation under heaven. And at this sound the multitude came together, and they were bewildered, because each one was hearing them speak in his own language.

> And they were amazed and astonished, saying, "Are not all these who are speaking Galileans? And how is it that we hear, each of us in his own native language? Parthians and Medes and Elamites and residents of Mesopotamia, Judea and Cappadocia, Pontus and Asia, Phrygia and Pamphylia, Egypt and the parts of Libya belonging to Cyrene, and visitors from Rome, both Jews and proselytes, Cretans and Arabians—we hear them telling in our own tongues the mighty works of God." And all were amazed and perplexed, saying to one another, "What does this mean?" But others mocking said, "They are filled with new wine."[10]

Some are bewildered, amazed, and astonished. Others mock. "They're drunk." An amazing thing happens next. Peter, whose last public act was to deny Jesus, stands on the southern steps of the temple, opens his mouth, and throws down the gauntlet. Peter in the garden of Gethsemane had a sword in his hand. Now he's got one in his mouth, and it may well be the best sermon ever given by a follower of Jesus.

> But Peter, standing with the eleven, lifted up his voice and addressed them: "Men of Judea and all who dwell in Jerusalem, let this be known to you, and give ear to my words. For these people are not drunk, as you suppose, since it is only the third hour of the day. But this is

what was uttered through the prophet Joel: 'And in the last days it shall be, God declares, that I will pour out my Spirit on all flesh, and your sons and your daughters shall prophesy, and your young men shall see visions, and your old men shall dream dreams; even on my male servants and female servants in those days I will pour out my Spirit, and they shall prophesy. And I will show wonders in the heavens above and signs on the earth below, blood, and fire, and vapor of smoke; the sun shall be turned to darkness and the moon to blood, before the day of the Lord comes, the great and magnificent day. And it shall come to pass that everyone who calls upon the name of the Lord shall be saved.'

"Men of Israel, hear these words: Jesus of Nazareth, a man attested to you by God with mighty works and wonders and signs that God did through him in your midst, as you yourselves know—this Jesus, delivered up according to the definite plan and foreknowledge of God, you crucified and killed by the hands of lawless men. God raised him up, loosing the pangs of death, because it was not possible for him to be held by it. For David says concerning him, 'I saw the Lord always before me, for he is at my right hand that I may not be shaken; therefore my heart was glad, and my tongue rejoiced; my flesh also will dwell in hope. For you will not abandon my soul to Hades, or let your Holy One see corruption. You have made known to me the paths of life; you will make me full of gladness with your presence.'

"Brothers, I may say to you with confidence about the patriarch David that he both died and was buried, and his tomb is with us to this day. Being therefore a prophet, and knowing that God had sworn with an oath to him that he would set one of his descendants on his throne, he foresaw and spoke about the resurrection of the Christ, that he was not abandoned to Hades, nor did his flesh see corruption. This Jesus God raised up, and of that we all are witnesses. Being therefore exalted at the right hand of God, and having received from the Father the promise of the Holy Spirit, he has poured out this that you yourselves are seeing and hearing. For David did not ascend into the heavens, but he himself says, 'The Lord said to my Lord, "Sit at my right hand, until I make your enemies your footstool."' Let all the house of Israel therefore know for certain that God has made him both Lord and Christ, this Jesus whom you crucified."

Now when they heard this they were cut to the heart, and said to Peter and the rest of the apostles, "Brothers, what shall we do?" And Peter said to them, "Repent and be baptized every one of you in the name of Jesus Christ for the forgiveness of your sins, and you will receive the gift of the Holy Spirit. For the promise is for you and for your children and for all who are far off, everyone whom the Lord our God calls to himself." And with many other words he bore witness and continued to exhort them, saying, "Save yourselves from this crooked generation." So those who received his word were baptized, and there were added that day about three thousand souls.[11]

FEARLESS

P eter and John are going to the temple for prayer at the ninth hour—about three in the afternoon. A man lame from birth is being carried to the gate of the temple called the Beautiful Gate where he was brought daily to beg alms. The man is over forty years old, so he's been doing this whole begging thing a long time. This is the sum of his life. His metal cup is worn, and his eyes glazed over with boredom and indifference. He rattles his cup at Peter, who looks down at him and says, "Look at us."[1] The man looks up, expecting money and nothing more. But Peter has something else in mind.

He says to the man, "I have no silver and gold, but what I do have I give to you. In the name of Jesus Christ of Nazareth, rise up and walk!" Then Peter grabs the lame man by the right hand, lifts him up, and "immediately his feet and ankles were made strong."[2]

The man erupts! He's dancing. Twirling. Hugging Peter and John. He is nearly out of his mind. Then he walks into the temple. He's been lame since birth, and according to Leviticus, "no one who has a blemish shall draw near, a man blind or lame."[3] He has been excluded from temple worship for his entire life. No fellowship with God. He has always been a complete and total outcast. But not any longer. Now he's included. A child of God. And he's jumping around in amazement, screaming and laughing at the top of his lungs. "And all the people . . . were filled with wonder and amazement at what had happened to him."[4]

The people are dumbfounded. Peter, not one to avoid a chance to preach, opens his mouth. "You killed Jesus. You denied the Holy Spirit. And faith in the name of Jesus has given this man perfect health. Therefore repent and turn back, that your sins may be blotted out."[5]

But anytime the Holy Spirit shows up, so does the enemy. So the priests, the captain of the temple, and the Sadducees burst onto the scene because Peter is teaching that in Jesus is the resurrection from the dead.

They arrest them, and as they are carted off to the prison, someone takes a head count. Another amazing thing has happened. "Many of those who heard the word believed, and the number of the men came to about five thousand."⁶ The church is growing.

The next day, the rulers, elders, and scribes gather along with Annas the high priest and Caiaphas. These are the men who killed Jesus. They bring in Peter and John, and ask a single question: "By what power or by what name have you done this?"⁷ So Peter, again not wanting to miss a chance to preach, lays down the gauntlet: "This Jesus is the stone that was rejected by you, the builders, which has become the cornerstone. And there is salvation in no one else, for there is no other name under heaven given among men by which we must be saved."⁸

The elders are skeptical, but they have one insurmountable problem: the healed man. He's standing there nodding. And no one can deny his healing because they've been stumbling over him for more than forty years. Unable to argue with the truth of what they're seeing, they command Peter and John to "speak no more to anyone in this name."⁹ Peter and John shrug, saying, "Whether it is right in the sight of God to listen to you rather than to God, you must judge, for we cannot but speak of what we have seen and heard."¹⁰

They release Peter and John, and all the believers lift their voices together and offer this prayer: "Now, Lord, look on their threats, and grant to Your servants that with all boldness they may speak Your word, by stretching out

Your hand to heal, and that signs and wonders may be done through the name of Your holy Servant Jesus."[11]

But then something happened.

"And when they had prayed, the place in which they were gathered together was shaken, and they were all filled with the Holy Spirit and continued to speak the word of God with boldness."[12]

BLINDED TO SEE

They call him "the Butcher." He has just returned from speaking with the high priest, where, "breathing threats and murder against the disciples,"[1] he asked for letters authorizing his campaign of extinction. Followers of Jesus have spread into Syria, and Saul is hunting them down, house to house, one by one. In his breast pocket, he is carrying those signed letters that he will use to drag followers of the Way out of their homes and return them to Jerusalem for trial. If they resist, he will behead them or run them through with a sword in the streets.

His reputation precedes him—a reputation built on, among other events, the stoning of a young convert named Stephen, during which Saul stood in smug, condescending agreement, holding the coats of those throwing stones. Now at his prime, his zeal is unmatched, as are his tactics and his thirst for violence. In truth, he is a terrorist. The worst of his kind. People live in abject terror because of him. He is singularly focused, a one-man killing machine. The high priest and council of elders will bear witness, Saul was on a mission to persecute the church of God beyond measure. To destroy it.[2]

A man of keen intellect and gifted mind, Saul had excelled rapidly and by the age of twelve had memorized the Torah. All five books. By heart. He then spent seven years studying and memorizing the Prophets. In his own words, "I advanced in Judaism beyond many of my contemporaries in my own nation, being more exceedingly zealous for the traditions of my fathers."[3]

Then came the Damascus road.

⊷⊷≡✦≡⊷⊷

Chin high, an arrogant air, the world at his feet, the Butcher of Tarsus is licking his chops. On the surface, it is an ordinary day, and he is traveling an ordinary road. Dusty. Big rocks. Potholes. A trade route. Lots of people come this way. The road on which Saul finds himself is just an everyday stretch of well-traveled highway.

But this is the day, and this is the road, on which God—once again—forever changes the course of human history. Following today, the world will never be the same.

Saul turns a corner and, without warning, without pre-lude, without introduction, God Most High has moved the sun from ninety million miles away to just a few feet in front of Saul's face. Blinded and disoriented, Saul falls to his knees. The definition of shock and awe. Struggling to breathe, Saul hears a voice say, "Saul, Saul, why are you persecuting Me?"[4]

Groveling, Saul manages a response: "Who are You, Lord?"

The Bright Morning Star, the One who upholds all things by the word of His power, responds with gentle kindness and abounding mercy: "I am Jesus, whom you are persecut-ing." Then Jesus says the most peculiar thing—a statement that suggests a history of interaction between Jesus and Saul to which we are not privy. The statement is unexpected, and it's as if Jesus pauses and ambles up alongside Saul, leaning over, whispering in his ear. A knowing tone in His voice. "It is hard for you to kick against the goads."[5]

Jesus has been sticking Saul for some time. Only Saul knows how long.

Saul stumbles off the road and spends three days without sight. No food. No water. His life, as he knows it, is over. Word of Saul's blindness spreads like wildfire and brings shouts of jubilation from the disciples and other followers of the Way.

Elsewhere in the town of Damascus there was "a certain disciple . . . named Ananias." Like the boy Samuel in the temple, Ananias answers, "Here I am, Lord."[6] He's beyond surprised God has tapped him on the shoulder. The Lord has a job for him: "Arise and go to the street called Straight, and inquire at the house of Judas for one called Saul of Tarsus, for behold, he is praying. And in a vision he has seen a man named Ananias coming in and putting his hand on him, so that he might receive his sight."[7]

Ananias scratches his head. "Umm . . . Lord, did You say *Saul*?"

"Yes."

"Of Tarsus?"

"Yup."

Long pause. "Are we talking about the same guy? I mean, the prisons and cemeteries are full of people he put there. Many don't have their heads. I'd like to keep mine where it is. Wouldn't it be better to just let him . . ."

The Lord continues, "Go, for he is a chosen vessel of Mine to bear My name before Gentiles, kings, and the children of Israel."[8]

Ananias rises, walks in obedience, lays hands on the blind Butcher, and says, "'Brother Saul, the Lord Jesus, who appeared to you on the road as you came, has sent me that you may receive your sight and be filled with the Holy Spirit.' Immediately there fell from his eyes something like scales, and he received his sight at once; and he arose and was baptized."[9]

Scales.

When Saul sat in the synagogue. Read the Law of Moses. Scorned Stephen. As he dragged children from their homes. Every time he kicked against the goads. Saul had been blind his whole life. But it wasn't until that dusty stretch of road that he was able to see his own blindness.

THE BANQUET OF THE AGES

The banquet hall is packed. Sounds of a party. Laughter. Forks on plates. A band. Dancing. Glow of a fire. Smell of fresh-baked bread. You're pressing your nose to the bottom window. Two feet off the ground. Outside looking in. Fogging up the glass. The night is cold, getting colder, and the rain has turned to sleet.

Inside there's standing room only. Oddly, everyone is barefoot and, unlike yours, their feet are beautiful. Somewhere in the back of your mind, you remember hearing stories of a gracious and kind King who fed His children at a table like that. A table of laughter and dancing and joy.

But that was before the fall.

You pull your toothpick legs and withered feet beneath you. A constant reminder. You glance at the doorkeeper.

He'll never let you in. And by law, you're not allowed. What were you thinking? That glass is the closest you'll ever get. You drag yourself into the darkness. Down the street that leads away.

In the darkness, you can hear the wolves tearing the flesh of those like you. The pack is devouring those not at the table. By now, they can smell you. You can hear them growling as you approach. It's not long now. A few more feet and they'll sink their teeth into your neck, choke your jugular, and drag you into the lair where they'll eat you while you watch. Maggots squirm around your fingers and the smell of rotting flesh curls your nose. This is not what you had imagined or even hoped, but this is where they'll devour you and cast your bones on the pile of the forgotten.

You turn, glance one last time at the banquet hall, and shake your head. Longing. That's when you feel the hot air on your neck. Hear the growl. You turn and gag at the stench of his breath. His face is caked with the blood of his last victim, and his smile confirms you are next. Behind him crouch two dozen more. They circle you, eyeing the tender flesh of your legs.

This is the end.

As the alpha wolf closes his massive mouth around your head, a bolt of light flashes from above you and sends the wolf rolling like a ball. When you open your eyes, a cloaked Man stands between you and the pack. Amid the flashes of light, wolves are flying everywhere. In seconds, they are gone. Only the whimpers remain.

In the silence, the Man towers over you.

You hide your face. You know better. Your kind is not allowed in the kingdom. Shame shadows your face. What were you thinking?

The Man stands over you, blocking your egress, proving you've been found out. Discovered. Your fate now will be worse than that of the wolves. The cold wind blows the sleet into your face and you shiver in the mud. You raise a hand to apologize, beg mercy, but it's no use. You've heard the stories. He's just; you're guilty. What could you possibly say? You're trespassing within the kingdom and on palace grounds. Men have been hanged for less. Even now you hear footsteps. Elite palace guards en route. Given your condition, they won't waste the death penalty on you. Following a speedy trial, they'll simply toss your body over the city wall where the wolves travel in packs and devour the rejected and the weak. The guards will stand atop the wall, warm themselves with drink and fire, and wager to see how long you'll last amid the carnage. How far you'll crawl before they consume you.

You are powerless.

As the *clank* of swords and shields grows closer, the Man kneels in the muck and mire, studying you. His face is veiled, but His countenance registers not anger but kindness. Relief, even.

You bury your face in the mud, hoping to elicit mercy. When you do, He lifts your chin. For a moment, He just stares, and you await the blow that never comes. Finally, with massive arms and without a word, He lifts you out of the mud, cradles your useless, noodle legs in His calloused hands, and strides toward the palace. The guards file in alongside. A perfect formation. An escort for the dying.

Approaching the massive door, the light shines on His hooded face. Silver-white hair. Emerald eyes. He's unlike any man you've ever seen. He commands, "Swing wide the gates!" and massive gears clank under their weight. While the gates are opened, He speaks. His voice sounds like a mountain stream or a gentle rain on the roof. "I've been waiting for you. I'm so glad you made it." He, too, is soaked to the bone, suggesting He's been standing in the night quite a while. Then He says the strangest thing. "I've missed you."

The words echo inside your mind. *Missed you.* And yet for an executioner you've never met, His hands are tender.

He pushes the hair out of your face and points inside. To the head table. "I've set a place for you." He shouts above to a figure standing at a window, surrounded by twenty-four guards dressed in resplendent armor. "Dad," the Man says, "we found him. And he has Your eyes."

The words *Your eyes* swim around inside you but find no place to rest.

The Man's gaze returns to you. A single shake of His head. "An amazing likeness." The dangling of your legs embarrasses you and you wish He'd set you down before the raucous laughter begins. You've grown accustomed to it. They always laugh when the sight of the grotesque is so comical.

When He steps inside, you are met by lights, warmth, and hushed voices. All eyes stare singularly at you and your soiled and torn rags and your impotent legs. Your pungent smell embarrasses you, but then again, how does a lame man relieve himself?

To the right is the hall of justice. Where the verdicts are handed down. Doors in the back lead the condemned to the gallows. To the left lies the banquet hall—and the smell of fresh bread and a wood fire.

Without pause, He turns left and parades you through long rows of smiling, clapping people. Certainly they are rejoicing at your capture and the coming verdict. He carries you to the head table where, rather than drop you where they can mock and spit, He places you in a seat next to His. Gently. The seat has your name on it. A band is playing music.

Until now the Man has been shrouded in cloak and hood and shadow. But inside the great hall, He removes it and shakes off the rain.

You are stunned. He is brilliant. Shining like the sun.

Dressed in white. It's the Prince. The Coming One. Heir to the throne. He turns, and through His linen shirt you can see the scars on His back. You've heard the stories. The legend of His capture, how they tortured Him, and the battle that ensued. How He, alone, defeated His captors and how before He returned to the palace, He emptied the prisons. Freeing those long held in chains and leading a host captive. Lastly, you know how He's spent His reign pursuing the wicked and returning for those still missing.

Knowing that you are wicked, you throw yourself to the floor and press your face to His feet. Begging mercy. Leniency. A quick death. Please.

He kneels again, lifts you quietly, and places you not in your seat but His. It's bigger. More room. He whispers, "Wait here."

The Prince is laughing. Exuberant. Spontaneously, He begins to dance, twirling the children who gather en masse around Him. Crowds throng the banquet hall and join in. The room is spinning with light and laughter and joy and the sound of melody. On the ceiling is a spinning disco ball made entirely of diamonds.

You sit in dumbstruck amazement as the Prince dances. He is not reserved. He is not collected. He is not proper.

You are undone.

The woman seated next to you whispers, "He's dancing for you."

This strikes you as absurd. "Why?"

She smiles. "Because He found you."

This, too, makes no sense. "Why was He looking?"

She laughs and waves her hand across the sea of people. "He always leaves the ninety-nine to find the one."

Aware of your singular unworthiness, you drop your head in shame, only to realize that your rags have somehow been replaced with corduroy—the cloth of the King. Your skin smells of mint, rosemary, lavender, and tea-tree oil, and all your putrid sores are gone. Amid the commotion, He returns to you, clinks His glass with His fork, and quiets the crowd. Silence falls.

"If I could have your attention please . . ." He puts His hand on your shoulder and points to a large blank wall where your picture appears on a screen equal to a hundred IMAX projectors. It's an old picture. Everyone can see it. They look from the wall to you and back to the wall. Your discomfort grows. The I'm-a-counterfeit-and-I-don't-belong-here uncertainty spreads across your face. You slump, hoping to slide beneath the table.

He continues, "Everyone, please welcome My guest of honor to dinner." Then He turns to you. Just you. You have the undivided attention of the Heir to the throne. Everything as far the eye can see or mind can imagine belongs to Him. He is undefeated in battle and He alone has done what none other could. He has no equal. He kneels. Eye level. He's whispering now. Just to you. "I'm so glad you made it. I watched you climb those steps out there and I was praying that you'd make it. That your faith would not fail." A tear rests in the corner of His eye. You've never seen joy this pure. This unadulterated. He stands, raises His glass. The applause is raucous.

More dancing erupts. The tables empty. Your eyes dart. You're not really comfortable. The sight of your feet draws you away. Ashamed, you pull the tablecloth over your lap. There must be some mistake. Mistaken identity. As soon as they uncover the truth, the party will stop and they'll leave you to the wolves. You await the laughter.

But He's not finished. He's clued into this—into you. Breaking ranks, He appears at your feet. He's kneeling. A bowl. Warm water. A towel. He pulls His hair into a pony- tail and peels back the tablecloth, holding your twisted feet in His hands. For a moment, He studies your scars where the bones once poked through the skin when you fell. Tracing them with His thumb, He shakes His head. "I know you've lived with this a long time. I'm so sorry this happened."

Tears spill off His face and land in the bowl. Slowly, He dips your mangled feet in the water. You recoil, but the water is warm and His hands so tender. Afraid but spurred by His smile, you take a chance, dip your feet in the bowl, and for reasons you can't explain, the Son of the King washes the maggots and manure off your feet. The kid sitting to your left, fist-deep in a ginormous bowl of chocolate ice cream, giggles with the most beautiful laughter, "He does that for everybody." He lifts his own spotless feet. "See mine?"

When the Son is finished, He says, "Wiggle for Me."

You haven't been able to wiggle your toes for years. You shake your head, "But Sire . . . I—"

He holds your feet in His hands. "Wiggle."

For the first time in memory, you wiggle your toes.

He chuckles. "Now your ankles."

You do, staring in dumbstruck amazement at ten beautiful toes, straight ankles, and muscled calves.

Your feet are beautiful on this mountain.

The look on your face brings joyous laughter from the Prince. But He pauses. Scratching His chin. He is staring at your chest. While He has fixed your feet, a deeper wound remains.

Without warning, He stands and the dance stops. All eyes on Him. He is of great renown and has many names. Faithful and true. Firstborn from among the dead. The One whose name is holy. He who holds the keys to death and hades. His eyes are fire, His hair white, and His voice sounds like rushing waters. His feet are burnished bronze— like one who walked through fire—and His sword is girded on His thigh. He is called the Lion and the Lamb, the Alpha and Omega, the First and the Last. He is radiant beyond understanding and He is the One who handcrafted your very feet from the dust. His soul is knit to yours.

This moment—this revelation, this healing, this banquet—this is why He brought you here. He is making good on the promise you thought was too good to be true.

He lifts you to your feet. Which is strange because you can't ever remember standing. Ever. You wobble, He catches you and sets you aright. Holding your hands, eye to eye, He speaks. "I want to correct a lie that was spoken to you long ago." He places His hand on your heart. "Erase its residue from your DNA." He lifts your chin. "You—" He inches closer, His breath blanketing you. Your eyes dart away. He smiles slightly. "Yes, you. I remember the day I made you. Fashioned you. You were then and are now perfect in every way. You are Mine. My chosen. And I will call you by name. You're heir to My throne. Co-ruler with Me. Everything that was stolen from you, I am returning. All that I have is yours. And I will feed you here. Forever."

The doubt rises and you shake your head. He's lost His mind. When He figures out He's got the wrong man . . . "But I'm not who You think."

Then He does the one thing only He could do. He calls you by your name. The name He gave you when He made you. The one written inside you.

You stammer. "But, what . . . how?"

He whispers one word: "*Tetelestai.*" It is finished.

At the sound of that one word, every person in the banquet hall falls to their knees, bows, and presses their palms to the ceiling. A sea of worship.

His Father appears. A pile of crowns at His feet. The Son walks you to His Father, presents you, and without hesitation, the Father launches Himself off His throne, wraps His arms around you, covers your face in kisses, and dresses you in a robe of matchless beauty.

You raise a finger. "How can this be?"

The Father points to the Son. He's waiting. He will not dance without you.

His foot is tapping. The music rises. He beckons. "Dance with Me."

Welcome to the Banquet of the Ages.

ENDNOTES

INTRODUCTION
1. John 3:14–15.
2. Luke 23:43.
3. John 14:6.
4. John 12:32.
5. Romans 3:26.
6. John 17:26.
7. Job 42:2, 5–6.
8. John 1:29.
9. Daniel 7:13 ESV.
10. 1 John 1:7.
11. Daniel 7:14.

CHAPTER 2: GOD WITH US
1. Revelation 4:3–5.
2. John 3:16.
3. Hebrews 1:2–3 NASB.
4. Colossians 1:16–17 NASB.
5. 1 Timothy 6:15–16 NASB.
6. John 1:2–5.
7. Revelation 1:8.

8. Revelation 3:14.

9. Revelation 5:5 NASB.

10. Ezekiel 28:12.

11. Hebrews 12:2 NASB.

12. John 17:14, 26, paraphrased.

13. Revelation 5:13.

14. Revelation 1:16.

15. John 1:1–2, 14.

16. Deuteronomy 6:4.

17. Luke 19:40.

18. Luke 1:32–33.

19. Isaiah 53; Psalm 22.

20. Malachi 4:2.

21. Luke 2:23.

22. Luke 2:14.

23. Isaiah 7:14.

24. Isaiah 9:2.

25. Philippians 2:6–8.

26. Isaiah 9:6–7.

CHAPTER 3: DAUGHTER OF GOD

1. Mark 5:1–20.

2. Mark 5:23.

3. Matthew 9:20–22; Mark 5:25–34; Luke 8:43–48.

4. Leviticus 15.

5. Malachi 4:2.

CHAPTER 4: ONLY BELIEVE

1. Luke 8:50 ESV.

2. Mark 5:41.

CHAPTER 5: IN THE POWER OF JESUS

1. Matthew 9:33.

2. Matthew 10:1.

3. Matthew 10:7–8.

4. Matthew 10:16–18, 22, 28.

5. Luke 9:6.

6. Luke 9:13.
7. Luke 9:35.
8. Luke 9:43.
9. Luke 10:3.
10. Luke 10:17–20.

CHAPTER 6: THE GOOD CONFESSION
1. Matthew 16:13.
2. Matthew 16:16.
3. Matthew 16:17–19.

CHAPTER 7: NEITHER DO I CONDEMN YOU
1. Hebrews 4:15.
2. John 8:10.
3. John 8:11.

CHAPTER 8: WHERE THE FATHER'S LOVE FOUND HIM
1. Proverbs 25:28.
2. Luke 15:15.
3. Proverbs 6:27.
4. Isaiah 64:6. By "rags," Isaiah meant used menstrual cloths. Let me spell this out. Left to our own devices, like our prodigal, the best we can produce absent a right relationship with the Father is no better than a bunch of used feminine products. That may offend you, but that's the point.
5. Luke 15:17.
6. Luke 15:20.
7. Luke 15:21.
8. Luke 15:24, paraphrased.

CHAPTER 9: THE SIGNATURE OF THE MESSIAH
1. Deuteronomy 34:3.
2. Joshua 2:11.
3. Mark 10:48.
4. Ezekiel 37:24.
5. Isaiah 11:1–2.
6. Luke 1:31–33.

ENDNOTES

7. Isaiah 29:18; 35:5 KJV.
8. Joel 2:32 KJV.
9. Psalm 146:8.
10. John 1:29.
11. Matthew 9:2.
12. Matthew 9:12–13.
13. Mark 10:51.
14. Psalm 139:15–16.
15. Luke 18:42.
16. Matthew 9:22; Mark 5:34; Luke 8:48.
17. Joshua 6:26.
18. Matthew 11:5.

CHAPTER 10: BY THIS . . .
1. Philippians 2:5–8.
2. Matthew 20:26–28.
3. John 13:15–16.
4. John 13:18; Psalm 41:9.
5. John 13:21.
6. John 13:25.
7. John 13:26.
8. John 13:27.
9. John 13:34.
10. John 13:34–35.
11. John 15:11–13.

CHAPTER 11: THE COVENANT
1. Luke 22:15–22 ESV.
2. John 13:27 ESV.
3. John 13:30.

CHAPTER 12: BETRAYED
1. 2 Samuel 15:30.
2. Matthew 26:36.
3. Matthew 26:38.
4. Matthew 21:9.
5. Luke 19:40.

6. Psalm 22:2.
7. Psalm 22:11.
8. Matthew 26:46.
9. Hebrews 1:2–3.
10. Isaiah 53:1–10, 12.

CHAPTER 13: KING OF THE JEWS

1. Numbers 21:9; John 3:14.
2. John 12:24.
3. Psalm 69:12.
4. Psalm 69:21.
5. Leviticus 17:11.

CHAPTER 14: THE FATHER'S SILENCE

1. Psalm 22:14.
2. Isaiah 52:14.
3. 2 Corinthians 5:21.
4. Isaiah 53:4.
5. Matthew 27:48.
6. Matthew 27:46.
7. Matthew 27:46.
8. In that culture, saying the first line and repeating the whole thing were essentially the same.
9. 2 Corinthians 5:21.
10. Roman crucifixions were routinely known to last twelve hours or more. It's why the soldiers broke the legs of the other two criminals hanging alongside Jesus.
11. Matthew 27:50.
12. John 19:30, paraphrased.

CHAPTER 15: PROPITIATION

1. Hebrews 10:20.
2. 1 Peter 3:18 NASB.
3. 2 Corinthians 5:21.
4. Revelation 4:1–11 ESV.
5. Isaiah 52:14.
6. Revelation 22:1–2.

7. Revelation 22:12 ESV.
8. Revelation 22:15 ESV.
9. Hebrews 8:6.
10. Revelation 19:11–16.
11. Revelation 21:5 ESV.
12. Revelation 21:6.
13. Revelation 21:3–27.
14. 1 Peter 3:18–20.
15. Daniel 7:9–14, paraphrased.

CHAPTER 16: ENTER THE KING OF GLORY

1. Hebrews 2:14.
2. 1 John 3:8.
3. Colossians 2:15.
4. Psalm 110:1–2.
5. Leviticus 17:11.
6. Romans 6:6, 14.
7. Isaiah 45:2.

CHAPTER 17: THE BORROWED TOMB

1. John 3:14.

CHAPTER 18: CAN IT BE?

1. John 18:11.
2. Matthew 27:4.
3. Matthew 27:4–5.
4. Acts 1:18–19 ESV.
5. Psalm 69:25; Acts 1:18–20.
6. Mark 16:1.
7. Luke 8:2–3.
8. Matthew 12:43–45.
9. Luke 24:5–6.
10. Luke 24:6–7.
11. Luke 24:8.
12. John 20:13.
13. John 20:15.
14. John 20:16.

15. John 20:17 ESV.
16. Psalm 31:5.

CHAPTER 19: ON THE ROAD TO EMMAUS
1. Luke 24:16–17.
2. Luke 24:18.
3. Luke 24:19–27 ESV.
4. Luke 24:28–29 ESV.
5. Luke 24:29–31 ESV.
6. Luke 24:31–35 ESV.

CHAPTER 20: THE DO-OVER
1. John 19:30.
2. John 21:5–6.
3. John 21:7.
4. Matthew 16:16.
5. John 21:10 ESV.
6. John 21:15.
7. John 21:18.
8. John 21:19.

CHAPTER 21: WHAT NEXT?
1. Genesis 22:8.
2. Isaiah 25:6–8.
3. Acts 1:6.
4. Acts 1:7–8.
5. Isaiah 6:2.
6. Revelation 19:1–6.
7. Acts 1:11.
8. Acts 1:8.

CHAPTER 22: THE HELPER COMES
1. John 14:16–19 ESV, emphasis added.
2. John 14:22.
3. John 14:23–26 ESV, emphasis added.
4. John 15:26–27 ESV, emphasis added.
5. John 16:7–10 ESV, emphasis added.

6. Luke 24:52–53.
7. Acts 1:13–14.
8. Exodus 23:17; 34:23.
9. Acts 2:1–4 ESV.
10. Acts 2:5–13 ESV.
11. Acts 2:14–41 ESV.

CHAPTER 23: FEARLESS

1. Acts 3:4.
2. Acts 3:6–7 ESV.
3. Leviticus 21:18 ESV.
4. Acts 3:9–10.
5. Acts 3:15–19, paraphrased.
6. Acts 4:4 ESV.
7. Acts 4:7.
8. Acts 4:11–12 ESV.
9. Acts 4:17 ESV.
10. Acts 4:19–20 ESV.
11. Acts 4:29–30.
12. Acts 4:31 ESV.

CHAPTER 24: BLINDED TO SEE

1. Acts 9:1.
2. Galatians 1:13.
3. Galatians 1:14.
4. Acts 9:4.
5. Acts 9:5.
6. Acts 9:10; 1 Samuel 3:4.
7. Acts 9:11–12.
8. Acts 9:15.
9. Acts 9:17–18.